# REA

## A MOST PRO

Isabelle took a long sip of coffee, peering at him over the rim of the porcelain bowl. Perhaps Madame would return with fresh coffee before politeness obliged her to go fetch it.

She had decided to forgive him for not having been solely and exclusively interested in her at first. After all, if fate had thrown them together, she could not argue with fate.

Nigel studied her, trying to read her thoughts. How was it possible that she could look so pretty in the morning? He had never known a woman who would even let him glance in her direction before noon.

Isabelle's pure complexion showed not a trace of paint or powder, and her splendid honey-colored hair was unconfined by a mobcap or ribbon.

All he had to do was reach across the table to touch it, draw its silken richness through his hand before he stroked her soft cheek and—hang it. He needed coffee very badly indeed.

The warmth of the sun was making him stupid. Was he to have nothing more than the fragrance of the stimulating drink he craved?

He set down his crust and stood up, walking to a bellpull hanging near the door. "Does this work in the fashion of the one in the dining room? I wish to summon the cook."

"Yes, it works. But the servants should not see us like this."

"Well, then I will hide under the table when they come."

She giggled, set down her bowl and licked a slight trace of milky coffee from her upper lip in a most provocative and annoying way. Nigel glared at her. . .

# BOOK YOUR PLACE ON OUR WEBSITE AND MAKE THE READING CONNECTION!

We've created a customized website just for our very special readers, where you can get the inside scoop on everything that's going on with Zebra, Pinnacle and Kensington books.

When you come online, you'll have the exciting opportunity to:

- View covers of upcoming books
- Read sample chapters
- Learn about our future publishing schedule (listed by publication month *and author*)
- Find out when your favorite authors will be visiting a city near you
- Search for and order backlist books from our online catalog
- Check out author bios and background information
- Send e-mail to your favorite authors
- Meet the Kensington staff online
- Join us in weekly chats with authors, readers and other guests
- Get writing guidelines
- AND MUCH MORE!

**Visit our website at
http://www.kensingtonbooks.com**

# THE BEAUTIFUL MISS MOUSEY

## LISA NOELI

**ZEBRA BOOKS**
**KENSINGTON PUBLISHING CORP.**
http://www.kensingtonbooks.com

ZEBRA BOOKS are published by

Kensington Publishing Corp.
850 Third Avenue
New York, NY 10022

All Kensington titles, imprints and distributed lines are
available at special quantity discounts for bulk pur-
chases for sales promotion, premiums, fund-raising, ed-
ucational or institutional use.

Special book excerpts or customized printings can also
be created to fit specific needs. For details, write or phone
the office of the Kensington Special Sales Manager: Kensington Publishing Corp., 850 Third Avenue, New York,
NY 10022. Attn. Special Sales Department. Phone: 1-800-
221-2647.

Zebra and the Z logo Reg. U.S. Pat. & TM Off.

First Printing: October 2004
10  9  8  7  6  5  4  3  2  1

Printed in the United States of America

# CHAPTER 1

*London, 1805*
*Within the walls of a Mayfair seraglio . . .*

"My dear nephew, I know I am thought quite mad. But hear me out."

Nigel Wollaston nodded and reclined upon the divan, resting one polished boot upon a stool in the shape of a fantastical mushroom. The old earl liked to talk, and the promised explanation threatened to be a long one.

The divan that did not quite accommodate Nigel's long body was made in the Moorish style and luxuriously upholstered in patterned silk. With opulent wall hangings and exotic bric-a-brac everywhere one looked, the drawing room very much resembled a harem's inner chamber, and his uncle's loose banyan robe and voluminous pantaloons brought to mind a sultan awaiting some indecent entertainment.

Indeed, the décor seemed eminently suitable for seduction in every way, Nigel thought. It was scarcely possible to sit upright upon Bertie's furniture. Female visitors, who could not sprawl comfortably as he was doing now, would simply slide to the floor.

As this polished surface was mostly covered with a gaudy carpet, plump silk cushions and tasseled bolsters, perhaps they would come to no harm, Nigel mused.

Bertie looked quite at home. He had once been ambassador to a distant land of Arabia whose borders shifted with the burning sands around it, and there he had acquired a taste for exotic women of dubious virtue and unmentionable skills, who liked to sit on floors.

And overstuffed objects of all kinds, Nigel thought, soft enough to sink into for hours. Soft enough to sleep upon—

"Nigel, my boy, do pay attention. You seem to be drifting off."

"My apologies, Uncle."

"As I was saying, a marriage at my age hardly seems necessary." He cleared his throat rather noisily. "No doubt you will ask why I do not simply acquire a mistress."

Bertie paused for rhetorical effect, obviously not expecting a reply to this statement, and stood to pace upon the carpet. He turned soon enough, having run out of room. His bachelor apartments at Albany Court were on the small side, though discreet and desirable, as advertised.

"I have found that mistresses are not worth the trouble. My last kept some lowborn lout on the side at my expense, according to her abigail."

Nigel gave him a quizzical look, not at all sure that he wanted to know the details.

His uncle continued to pace. "I had the foresight to bribe the girl in advance for the information. I was concerned for my health, you see, and the mistress in question was a liar."

Nigel hid a smile. His uncle was much given to hypochondria, which did not keep the old man from enjoying the company of frivolous females.

"Have you never told a lie, Uncle?"

"I have told dozens—but not about matters of health. My boy, the great pox is prevalent these days, and we cannot blame the French for it indefinitely."

"A reasonable concern, Uncle. The mercury cure gives a man the shakes, but it is not effective."

Bertie nodded, looking suitably grave, though there was a twinkle in his eye. "Therefore, I should prefer a wife."

"Wives are not always faithful."

"Thank you, Nigel. Your wisdom is commendable, considering your inexperience. You have never married."

"Neither have you. Wives are no less expensive than mistresses. A countess is obliged to keep up appearances."

"Of course. And I have no doubt that my little dove will furnish her nest in fine style."

"Are you referring to Miss Phoebe Sharpe?"

"I am. And I shall be happy to indulge her innocent whims, for I am very fond of her. She seems delightfully unspoiled."

*Little dove? Unspoiled?* Odd words indeed to describe that particular female, Nigel thought. He clapped a hand over his forehead to hide his eyebrows, which had risen into his hair.

"Do you have a headache, Nigel? I have an excellent remedy—"

"No, I do not. But thank you for your concern. Is Miss Sharpe to become your wife? She is young, Uncle."

The earl smiled broadly and rather wickedly. "She knows what she wants and she is old enough to marry."

"I see." Nigel had no idea whether to offer congratulations or commiseration.

"I have asked Bishop Freamington for a special license so that we may marry at any time and place we choose. Dear old Freamy. We were at Cambridge together, you know. He was more than a match for me in those days, bottle for bottle and wench for wench. Nothing like a solid classical education, my boy."

Nigel nodded absentmindedly. "Concerning this marriage—does Miss Sharpe, ah, return your affections?"

"Marriage is a financial transaction, Nigel, not a romantic one. She is eager to trade her youth and beauty to live in luxury and acquire a great name, and I . . ." The old man trailed off.

Nigel waited.

"I shall see some pretty scenery, my boy. And furthermore . . ."

Nigel barely listened to whatever he said next.

Apparently his uncle knew nothing of the talk at White's regarding that pretty scenery. An idiotic bet had been proposed but not entered in the book. Some idle fellow had wondered if Phoebe owed her eye-catching décolletage to the uplifting undergarment known as the Invisible Arrangement—and another had asked if all that soft flesh was really Sharpe and laughed uproariously at his own wit.

By all reports, no one had yet been foolish enough to stake money on finding out the answer. Nigel supposed that the information could be begged or bought from Miss Sharpe's corsetière, a mysterious Frenchwoman named Madame Zazou, if it came to that.

Though he sincerely hoped to see his uncle contentedly married, he had to assume that the infatuation would end soon enough, with the usual tears and recriminations and flying china that marked the finale of most love affairs.

However, if the baggage—if Miss Sharpe—made Bertie truly happy, then perhaps it was meant to be. They might well be wed before the season drew to a close.

How curious it would be to have an aunt twelve years younger!

He would have to make the best of it—certainly he was extremely fond of his uncle, who had been like a father to him. And Nigel would not stand in their way. *Let me not to the marriage of true minds admit*—oh, what was it that should not be admitted? The exact words of the sonnet escaped him at the moment.

"Dear boy, have you heard one word I said?"

Nigel forced his mind back to his uncle. "Yes. You were speaking of . . . scenery."

The earl harrumphed. "Just as I thought. You were not paying the slightest attention when I changed the subject. I was speaking of the Wollaston hunt."

"Indeed." Nigel did his best to look interested, though he had no interest whatsoever in hunting and its attendant cacophony of beagles and bugles.

His sympathies lay entirely with the fox, which he admired for usually getting the better of the unruly horde that pursued it.

At the last such event in which he had been obliged to participate, he had made an early escape down a shady lane, along with his grateful mount.

Shortly thereafter, he had been surprised to spy in a clearing a crimson-furred vixen with legs so neat and black she appeared to be wearing stockings. She had evidently doubled and tripled back, successfully leading the horses and hounds to empty earths in order to fetch her waiting cubs safely from their den.

Such feminine cunning and maternal courage in a mere animal had convinced Nigel to leave well enough alone forever. But hunting was another passion of his uncle's and, for the sake of politeness, he strove to give at least the appearance of listening now.

"Your father is leading the hunt this year. He has invited me down to the country next week, to admire his new saddle or some such thing, though it is early spring and many months before fox-hunting season begins. He plans a practice run for one and all."

Nigel grinned. "A stable lad on a fast horse will drag something vile for the pack to follow."

"A brush, of course—provided by the last fox unfortunate enough to get caught. But most of the participants will end the day with nothing to show for it but bruises and muddy faces."

"Will you go alone, Uncle?"

"No. Miss Sharpe shall accompany me."

Indeed, thought Nigel with amusement. His father, Lord Charles, openly disapproved of his older brother's entanglement with Phoebe Sharpe.

Her bloodlines were good enough—Lord Charles tended to speak of such things in breeder's terms, as if the lady in question were simply another beagle—the Sharpes were descended from an old line of the Sussex squirearchy. And the girl was certainly in the pink of health.

Phoebe might well produce an heir and a spare, despite Bertie's advanced years. Meaning that Lord Charles would never be an earl, only an Honorable, for the rest of his days—not that it mattered to his only son.

Charles Wollaston, an intemperate man given to fits of red-faced fury, had harried Nigel's gentle mother into an early grave and Nigel saw no reason to ever forgive him for that or his many other sins.

"I expect you will find much to amuse you, Uncle. But I shall not attend."

"I understand." The old man stopped pacing and settled into a capacious striped armchair big enough for two sultans, folding his hands across his round belly. "I hope your father will make Miss Sharpe feel welcome in our family. Have you ever seen her, my boy?"

"Yes," said Nigel slowly. "In passing. She seems to be"—he paused, trying to think of a polite way to describe Phoebe—"a woman of surprising charm." Two surprising charms, to be exact.

The older man leaned back and put his bowed legs up upon a tufted stool, favoring a gouty toe on his left foot.

"Just so, Nigel. I see no reason to spend my remaining years alone, and Miss Sharpe is pleasant company."

"Do you love her, Uncle?" It was a forward question, but one that Nigel felt compelled to ask.

His sophisticated companions derided the notion of romantic passion even as they racked up conquests by the score, but Nigel secretly wondered about it. His own *affaires de coeur* had been numerous and varied, but that vital organ, his heart, had remained essentially untouched. Yet surely the wondrous feeling so celebrated by poets and playwrights existed, even if he had not experienced it thus far.

"Love? What has love to do with it?" Bertie replied after a moment's thought.

Nigel noted a fleeting look of tenderness in his uncle's eyes that belied the older man's cynical words. "It was an idle question—nothing more."

"Why do you ask, my boy? Are you in the grip of that powerful emotion? Prepare to abandon your reason if so."

"Certainly not."

His uncle gave him a shrewd glance. "Yet you have fallen into unexplained reveries several times in the space of an hour. And you have a moony look in your eyes. I suspect the worst."

"It is spring. That is all."

"Ah. So that is what has intoxicated you."

"I am not intoxicated by anything—and if I seem distracted, it is because the room is too warm. Do you mind if I open a window?"

"No, no, not at all," Bertie said affably as Nigel jumped up. "You must try Dr. Greene's Special Stimulating Powder for Relief of Cerebral Disturbances. It is most helpful for absentmindedness."

Nigel lifted the sash as high as it would go. "I prefer strong coffee, Uncle. The so-called Dr. Greene is a notorious quack and his powder is nothing more than snuff."

"Still, I believe in it. And I have put a substantial sum into the company," Bertie said, a little peevishly. "Dr. Greene said I should triple my money in a twelvemonth."

Nigel scowled as he looked out the window, his hands clasped behind his back. "It is not a wise investment. Have I not explained that—"

"Oh, bother my investments," Bertie replied. "You never used to be so serious, Nigel. Have you lost your appetite for fun? What happened to the dashing devil who caught the eye of every woman? Just like myself in my salad days, eh? Before I grew so stout!"

He slapped his belly as if that might make it disappear, then twisted in his chair to look at—his nephew's back. The younger man did not turn around and did not reply.

"Oh, never mind, Nigel. I do appreciate your efforts on my behalf. Your careful management of my financial affairs has put a hundred thousand pounds in the hands of my various creditors, damn and blast them all. Wollaston Hall and its lands are no longer encumbered by debt. How did you do it?"

Nigel only shrugged and continued to look out the window. "I can add and subtract and figure out percents." He caught a glimpse of a graceful young woman on the street below, whom he thought he had seen before, though he could not remember precisely where. A golden-haired boy in a short jacket walked by her side, carrying a basket.

Her dress was of lustrous gray silk that shone in the sunlight and a pretty bonnet hid her face, which he wished very much to see. But she and her young companion walked on, under trees just turned the tender green of early spring, and were soon lost to view.

"You are too modest, my boy. Your decisiveness and your intelligence are nothing short of remarkable. I suspect you shall be a rich man someday, with a fine house of your own."

"Perhaps."

"Though it has been most amusing, not to say convenient, having you in the apartments next door," Bertie said almost wistfully.

"But the baron who rented them to me is returning from the Continent."

The old earl nodded. "Yes. He has a new mistress who wishes to avoid her Parisian creditors, according to Jeremy Gresham, who knows everybody and everything."

Nigel smiled slightly. "So he does. Dear old Jem."

"My boy, you shall not be cast upon the street—simply move in with me until you are ready to establish a household of your own. I will see to it that—"

"Oh, I shall find a place to stay, never fear." Nigel craned his neck, eager to see if the young woman in gray would emerge at the corner of the secluded street. She did not—but a sweet breeze came through the window, dispelling the oppressive atmosphere of the room and lifting his spirits.

He strode to his uncle's chair and patted him on

the shoulder. "I must take my leave. Shall we dine together tonight?"

Bertie looked at him sadly. "Alas, no. I cannot indulge in certain of life's sweetest pleasures. My physician has restricted me to beef broth and dry bread."

"Then I shall dine at my club. Good-bye, Uncle."

"Good-bye. Count yourself fortunate to be young, Nigel. And do close that window. The draft will be the death of me."

Nigel grinned and shut it firmly before he left the room.

# CHAPTER 2

*Several weeks prior to Nigel's conversation with his
uncle, the following events occurred . . .*

"Isabelle, you must marry."

"Why?"

Lady Griselda pushed her spectacles higher on
her aristocratic beak and pursed her lips. "Because
every girl must marry, and does marry, unless she
is exceptionally ugly or too old. You are neither and
your lineage is distinguished. Consider the noble
branches of your family tree—"

Isabelle sighed. "Yes, Aunt. They want nothing
to do with an impoverished twig."

"True, you have no fortune, but others have married without one. Improve yourself, Isabelle. Curl
your hair and dash on a bit of rouge."

Lady Griselda was a firm believer in such improve-
ments at any age—in fact, her bobbing ringlets and
scarlet cheeks made her look like a painted doll, in

Isabelle's opinion. Her coquettish appearance was not at all what one might expect from the mistress of so grand and gloomy a house as the Priory.

Built in imitation Gothic style, the Priory had been called one of the prettiest dungeons in England by an esteemed critic of architecture, now dead. It boasted nineteen bedrooms, though a few lacked roofs, as well as parlors, drawing rooms, halls, corridors, and paneled chambers by the score.

The parlor they presently occupied was damp and dismal, and much of its ornamental plasterwork ceiling had crumbled. But Lady Griselda refused to spend her considerable fortune on anything as mundane as repairs.

It was the only home Isabelle had ever known, as her parents had died in her infancy and she had no other living relations. She was not quite sure that Lady Griselda actually was a relation but she called her Aunt anyway.

"You ought to dampen your dresses, gel. Everyone does it." Griselda waggled a finger and her ringlets bounced in time with it.

Isabelle concentrated on her embroidery and tried not to smile, surprised that the aged woman had even heard of this quirk of fashion. Griselda must be very eager indeed to marry her off.

The revelatory effect of damp, clinging muslin might cause certain prudish young curates to swoon dead away, Isabelle thought. She had endured afternoon tea with many since reaching her eighteenth year—her great-aunt would not hold a dance and curates did not seem to dance, in any case. In fact, they were wont to disapprove of anything that ordinary mortals enjoyed.

Nonetheless, Lady Griselda encouraged them, perhaps hoping that one might ask for Isabelle's hand, expecting to be granted the living and the rectory that came with the vast estate in Surrey. Apparently there were no other eligible men for miles around, and there never had been.

The thought was most discouraging.

Isabelle could not count the elderly professor who had lived alone in the crumbling gamekeeper's cottage ever since she could remember, until his recent death. The snowy-haired Dr. Inchbald was another relation of Lady Griselda's and also poor, according to that worthy woman, who liked to put people in their place.

Long retired from Oxford, he had served as Isabelle's tutor in lieu of rent, teaching her Latin, Greek, the use of the globe and atlases, and centuries of English history.

Every now and then, he would unroll one or another of his many maps of London, tracing the streets, ancient and new, with a shaking finger and recounting his youthful adventures there.

As a result, she knew the city well—or at least as well as she knew the small village a few miles from the Priory. She had never been anywhere, really, though books—she was always reading—provided glimpses of bigger places and other worlds.

The professor, whose mother was French, had drilled her in that language, which Lady Griselda thought unnecessary. And while he had napped with his cat—he and this affectionate animal snored and purred in perfect harmony—his intelligent young pupil had been happy to amuse herself with a cache of French novels, left behind by an elegant female cousin making a hasty escape from Griselda's grim abode.

But there was no one to speak French with now, since Dr. Inchbald died peacefully a few months ago, Isabelle thought sadly. She did miss the dear old professor—

She glanced up, suddenly aware of Lady Griselda's penetrating stare. That lady seemed to choose her next words very carefully. "As I said, you must marry. And you are a penniless orphan, so you must marry well."

Isabelle nodded. She had heard this speech before—many times.

"And my prospects will be better in London, as you have so often pointed out."

Lady Griselda waved a hand, almost upsetting her porcelain teacup. "The great metropolis awaits!"

The prospect of getting rid of her young ward seemed to charge the old lady with something very like enthusiasm, Isabelle noticed.

Griselda continued. "The duke—dear Oswald—has had my letter for some time, so we can assume that he is expecting you. As I remember, his house is very grand and you will be provided with every comfort, Isabelle, as well as social entrée."

"Yes, Aunt. I am much obliged to you."

Dear Oswald was nearly ninety and deaf as a post, or so Isabelle understood. She had also inadvertently learned, from the whispered gossip of the older servants, that the thrice-married duke and the prim Griselda had once been lovers—long, long ago.

Griselda peered at Isabelle over her spectacles. The gel was stitching a pious maxim concerning the duties of women onto a piece of taut linen.

Well and good. She should know her duties, considering that her station in life might be a humble one. If she could not be married off, she would have to become a governess. Certainly Professor Inchbald had educated her sufficiently for that.

Nonetheless, Isabelle was passably pretty, even to Griselda's critical eyes, and might do well enough for herself during the Season, once she made her debut. The old lady intended to ask the duke to present Isabelle at Court and she was sure he would agree.

Griselda heartily disliked travel, and the girl had no living relatives to perform this necessary introduction into polite society. She congratulated herself silently once again for resolving the all-important matter of the debut so neatly.

What if Isabelle became the toast of the *ton* after all? Engaged to—the old lady could already envision the engraved announcement, done in splendid curlicues—a Peer of the Realm. Or an Eminent Personage of Sterling Reputation, if no peer was to be had.

She had assured Isabelle several times over the last few months that the august duke had impeccable social connections and a prodigious brain, not to mention membership in a famous scientific academy, the Royal Society for Polar Exploration.

Isabelle had been unimpressed. According to a yellowed scandal sheet she had found—another relic of the lady who had left the French novels—the brave explorers were famous chiefly for dozing off in armchairs before a roaring fire at their club on St. James Street.

Knowing nothing of this information, her great-aunt had pointed out that the duke was certain to introduce her to many wealthy and titled men, who might even be persuaded to marry her between expeditions to the ends of the earth.

Isabelle had swallowed a laugh upon hearing this preposterous declaration—but she *had* wanted to go to London and agreed to Lady Griselda's plan with enthusiasm. Dresses, shoes, cloaks, bonnets, and all manner of accoutrements had been ordered, made to measure, and finally delivered just yesterday.

She was to leave on the morrow. The thought was thrilling and made up for any number of curates.

"Once you are properly launched into society, I shall resume my work on behalf of the poor. Ungrateful wretches."

The younger woman paused to thread a needle and did not look at her. Lady Griselda emitted a heartfelt sigh.

"As you know, Isabelle, I intend to build a new poorhouse but the current inhabitants refuse to move from the old one."

Perfectly understandable, in Isabelle's opinion. The site of the planned poorhouse was miles away, far from any chance of gainful employment and the humble comforts of village life. But there was no use in pointing that out to someone as self-righteous as Lady Griselda.

"I have asked the new vicar for his spiritual support and we are to pray for divine guidance in the matter. He is unmarried and not unattractive, as you know, Isabelle. If you would join us—" She looked hopefully at her great-niece, who kept her eyes upon her needlework.

"Thank you, Aunt," Isabelle said firmly, "but no."

The new vicar, whose receding chin and gooseberry-colored eyes repelled her, had already been discussed as a marital prospect—one that Isabelle had declined immediately.

Lady Griselda shook her head disapprovingly. "As you wish. I have promised to provide his favorite delicacy, turtle soup, if Cook can be persuaded to slaughter the turtle."

Isabelle knew that the soft-hearted cook would do no such thing. Dear Mrs. Pursley had made a vow "to return the hunfortunate creature to its briny ocean 'ome." She had let it loose in the garden in the meantime and the turtle had taken up residence beneath a tangle of briers where no one could get at it.

"If not, then we shall have plaice," Lady Griselda said brightly. "Did I tell you of the new vicar's jest regarding this very fish? *There is a time and a plaice for everything.* Such a clever man—"

"Indeed. Please ask Mrs. Pursley to send up my supper on a tray when he arrives. I am beginning to feel slightly unwell." That was a lie but Isabelle had absolutely no wish to meet the vicar again.

Isabelle's first journey beyond the glorious countryside of Surrey began badly. The hired coachman, a stranger with a bristling black beard, arrived very late, driving a rattletrap equipage splashed with mud. The day was drawing to a gloomy close. Dark clouds above threatened rain and the sun was sinking fast.

Mrs. Pursley, who had neglected her kitchen duties to run out and say a proper good-bye, was scowling at him, her dear, pugnacious face set in a thousand wrinkles.

"I don't like the looks of that hanimal. Hemploy the humbrella if he dares to trifle with ye, Miss Isabelle. Thrust 'ere—and 'ere." She demonstrated this action with a rolling pin and glared at the sullen coachman a few yards away, who took no notice of her or Isabelle.

"Never fear. I shall defend myself to the death," the young woman assured her gravely.

"And write often—do. Oh, Miss Isabelle! The Priory will not be the same without you."

Mrs. Pursley embraced her with deep affection before Isabelle clambered into the back of the carriage.

She was hampered by a stiff new traveling costume consisting of a woolen gown, spencer, bonnet, gloves, and shoes so pretty that she could scarcely walk in them; but she wedged herself in somehow, between the portmanteaux, valises, parcels, and cases that had not fit outside and under. The arrangement was most uncomfortable, but there was nothing to be done.

At least Isabelle did not have to share the cramped space with the chaperone, a retired governess whose blue-blooded charges had long ago grown up and gone to the devil despite her constant admonitions to the contrary. The woman had never arrived.

A village lad had been sent to fetch her straightaway and had returned with a gracefully penned note that claimed she was ill. Isabelle suspected that there had been some quibble over her fee. Lady Griselda hated to pay for anything in advance—or afterwards. The old lady trilled her good-byes from an upper window and shut it quickly as the rain began to fall.

Truly, thought Lady Griselda, her kindness to so distant a relative was quite remarkable—and quite enough. She hoped in her heart of hearts that Isabelle would not return.

Lady Griselda tugged vigorously at the bellpull for Mrs. Pursley, who could not hear the summons or see her imperious mistress. The cook was waving the rolling pin at Isabelle, along with a large handkerchief, stopping now and then to wipe her eyes with the handkerchief.

Lady Griselda tugged again, harder, ripping the ribbon bellpull from the wall. She spluttered with outrage. There was no one about to blame, which made her even crosser.

Isabelle peered out the small window and waved once more to Mrs. Pursley as the wheels of the hired coach began to roll.

"Good-bye, miss! Good-bye!"

"Good-bye, Mrs. Pursley!"

The white handkerchief fluttered forlornly as the plump cook watched the coach slowly roll down the gravel drive, then gather speed.

Isabelle leaned back when the coach suddenly jerked forward, letting her thoughts drift until they reached the crossing. The road to London was to the left, and the rain had turned the ruts into deep puddles.

After an hour, perhaps less—the brooding sky and rain-splattered window made it impossible for her to guess the time—she was jolted into near-insensibility and nodded off.

She awakened only once during the time that followed, hearing the coachman's coarse voice singing rather drunkenly, something about Nellie Nye and Nancy-o and a sailor they both liked. She soon fell asleep again.

The resounding clatter of ironbound wheels over cobblestones brought her back to her senses.

Isabelle peeped out of the carriage window. Had they arrived in London so soon? And was this Mayfair? The houses she saw were elegant indeed, built of light-colored stone and surrounded by railings of wrought iron. The duke's house was across from Grosvenor Square, she knew. Was that the shadowy, rain-drenched park that they had just passed?

She rapped upon the roof of the coach with her rolled-up umbrella but the driver did not seem to hear it.

Here and there, street lamps cast flickering light onto handsome façades, but there was no one, not even a night watchman, to be seen in the driving rain.

Very well—chaperone or no, she would soon be safely indoors with dear Oswald. She assumed there would be numerous servants to assist her and perhaps an elderly gentlewoman for companionship, if the duke's house was even half as grand as Lady Griselda had claimed.

She braced herself against the squabs as the coachman suddenly pulled up in front of a particularly magnificent house. Its classical pediment was supported by Corinthian columns—at least she thought they were Corinthian.

She tried to remember which was which, so she could compliment the duke upon his taste. The

Doric were the plain ones, and Ionic the scrolly ones, so these must be Corinthian—oh, what did it matter? All she wanted was to be inside.

The weary horses stamped and snorted, shaking their jingling harnesses. No doubt they, too, were hoping for a warm, dry place to rest tonight, Isabelle thought. They certainly deserved a good measure of oats as well, but she had her doubts that the rough man who drove them would provide it.

He jumped down with a curse, opened the coach door, and peered inside. Isabelle was scrambling over the heap of bags to make her escape.

"There ye be. Come along." He stretched out his dirty hand to Isabelle and assisted her out rather roughly. Then he clambered back up to his box, muttering into his bristly black beard—something about the difficulty of the journey and there not being enough money in the wide world for all his trouble.

"Oh—my umbrella, if you please—I dropped it within the coach and it is raining."

"So it is," he said sarcastically. "And I am wetter than ye, miss."

The oaf made no move to fetch it but sat where he was, huddled in his soaked greatcoat with a morose expression on his face. He tipped a cloudy glass bottle to his lips and swilled the dregs of a brown liquid from it.

"I must have my umbrella—"

He interrupted her. "I heard ye. But I 'aven't been adequately recompensated as of yet. Her ladyship give me only 'alf. Said ye'd pay the rest."

Isabel gave an exasperated sigh and searched her reticule, standing close to the coach for what little shelter it provided from the driving rain. Surely there was a guinea or two within its silk folds—no, there were none. Lady Griselda, who counted every coin twice and bit them afterward, had somehow forgotten to include so much as a tuppence.

However, the old lady had put in a sugar-bun left over from breakfast and wrapped it in the paper on which she had written the duke's address. The stale bun crumbled at Isabelle's touch as she pulled out the paper, trying to read Griselda's shaky script.

She looked at the number on the paper, then at the magnificent house. The address was correct, Number 17—but why were the windows so dark? She turned her attention to the more pressing matter of paying the coachman.

"I have no money. But when you return to the Priory—"

The drunken coachman belched and glared at her. Then he bellowed a curse that froze her to the marrow and howled with rage at the unfairness of a world that had made him a coachman and not a lord—or, at the very least, an innkeeper.

"See here—" Isabelle began, adopting Lady Griselda's most imperious tone—but that only seemed to make him angrier.

Without another word, he gave the horses' rumps a stinging slap with the wet reins and careened away down Grosvenor Street toward Soho.

She stood there for a moment, gaping like a ninny—and was thoroughly drenched within seconds. The tremendous spray from the carriage wheels and pounding hooves prevented her from following him.

Furious, powerless, Isabelle took off a shoe and

hurled it with all her might in the general direction in which he had disappeared.

The filthy sot had taken everything she owned in the world!

No doubt he would sell it all and squander his ill-gotten gains in some low tavern. She hoped he would be poisoned, she hoped he would swallow a cockroach with his sour ale, she hoped—oh, it was no use. A mongrel dashed out of a side street and ran away with the shoe. She deeply regretted throwing it but was distracted within seconds when her bonnet blew off.

Isabelle limped up the stairs of the duke's town house before she thought to take off the remaining shoe. There. She was standing straight, not listing to one side like a sinking ship, and ready to explain everything to the servant in livery who would answer. She patted her hair in vain—it was coming down and stuck unpleasantly to the back of her neck.

But there was no reply, no sound of measured footsteps, when she knocked upon the door, scowling at the lion's-head knocker, which held the thick ring of brass in a scowl of its own.

Several minutes passed. A desperate inquiry made of an old man who happened by elicited the information that the ancient duke had been dead and buried for two years. Another important detail Lady Griselda had forgotten to confirm, evidently.

More wet than she had ever dreamed it was possible to be, she considered bursting into tears but decided against it, as it would only make her wetter.

She leaned over the iron railing to peer into a window and saw only the indistinct shapes of furniture draped in dusty white cloths and, very faintly, the webs of countless spiders. She dismissed the idea of climbing inside. Isabelle hated spiders.

Perhaps she could take refuge in a church and ask for assistance from some kind soul. Mrs. Pursley, a devout churchgoer who cherished an unconfirmed belief in the goodness of all mankind, assuredly would have advised her to do just that.

But where was the nearest church?

Slipping her shoe back on—at least one foot would be somewhat protected from the cobblestones and mud—Isabelle walked down the stairs and into the streets, barely glancing at the few people out in the deluge, all of them men. Surely they had no reason to look at her with such brazen fascination. Had they never seen a wet woman before?

Then a swiftly moving shadow, no bigger than a boy, came toward her. She looked down when the shadow brushed past to see that it had cut the strings of her reticule and taken it.

Isabelle now had good reason to be frightened. She was alone and lost in a strange city, set upon by thieves, who would soon find out that they had stolen only a stale sugar-bun and return, enraged, to finish her off. Or hold her for ransom. Not that Lady Griselda would pay it without making a dreadful fuss.

She headed south on Audley Street, walking briskly despite her soaked clothes. After some minutes, she stopped to consider where she was going— she had not the least idea—then turned abruptly and stepped hard upon the booted foot of a woman dressed all in black, holding a black, deeply fringed umbrella.

Isabelle very nearly tripped over the small brown-and-white dog on a lead at the woman's side.

The mysterious stranger gave Isabelle a contemptuous look and brushed a black-gloved hand against the sleeve that Isabelle's dripping spencer had touched.

"Oh, I am dreadfully sorry—do please excuse me—but the rain—" Isabelle took a deep breath. "If I might introduce myself—I am Miss Mousey. Miss Isabelle Mousey."

"And I am Madame Zazou."

The other woman's voice was pleasingly soft and her accent elegant, Isabelle noted. She racked her brain for the right words, her fluent French momentarily escaping her. The professor had never prepared her for a situation like this.

"Ah! *Bonjour!* Hello! *Comment-allez vous?* How are you?" That was quite wrong. She should have said *bon soir*—good evening—not *bonjour*—good day—and she certainly should have inquired sympathetically about Madame's toes and apologized.

"*Bien.*" The older woman shrugged and smiled slightly. "Your accent is good. Do you know the language well, mademoiselle? So many English have but a few words of it and they mispronounce those." She extended her fringed silk umbrella ever so slightly over Isabelle's head as she shrewdly assessed her bedraggled but very fine clothes from head to toe.

The girl was a beauty, with fine features and striking honey-colored hair, Madame noticed. And she was obviously not long from the schoolroom, with an innocent look in her brown eyes that reminded Madame of her own younger sister.

But why was she out upon the streets on such a

night? Madame decided to wait for the girl to explain.

Isabelle pulled her stocking-clad foot under her dress and thrust out the shod one, trying once more to stand up straight.

"Mademoiselle, where is your other shoe?"

"I threw it at the coachman—and I have been robbed—and the duke is dead—to say nothing of the spiders, though they are very much alive!" She burst into tears at last.

Perhaps that was the explanation—the girl was a lunatic. But Madame Zazou did not think so and waited another few moments for the girl to calm herself. She reached into the small beaded bag that swung at her wrist and found an exquisite handkerchief edged in lace, which she gave to Isabelle.

"What shall I do, Madame? I am alone and I am lost." She wiped her eyes.

The Frenchwoman thought it over. "You are distraught—and you cannot remain upon the street, mademoiselle. It is not respectable. And it is raining very hard indeed. Come. Walk with me." She extended a gloved hand.

Isabelle wondered what Madame herself was doing upon the streets at this ungodly hour. She had secretly read lurid tales—belonging to Mrs. Pursley—of the bawds and pimps of London, perhaps the most interesting part of her somewhat haphazard education over the years.

Was Madame Zazou a—a procuress? The older woman did have the air of someone coming from a clandestine assignment. And had Madame taken Isabelle for a country girl, ready to sell her maidenhood to the highest bidder? She had better explain—but what if Madame misunderstood? She could not remember the French word for maiden-hood, if indeed she had ever known it.

The older woman seemed to be waiting for Isabelle to answer. Perhaps Madame Zazou had returned from a midnight rendezvous with a noble lover, Isabelle thought wildly, though she knew from the novels she had devoured that great men gave their mistresses carriages, horses, diamonds, gowns, et cetera—but Madame was plainly if elegantly dressed and on foot.

Madame smiled slightly, as if reading her mind. "Do not be afraid. I am only a corsetière. A stay-maker, to use the English phrase. The girls I employ are honest seamstresses, nothing more. And you are welcome in my house for the night. Or longer, if you wish to work."

Isabelle heaved a sigh of relief.

"*Merci,* Madame. You are most kind. I can sew a little or—" She searched her mind desperately for useful skills that would not compromise her reputation, which seemed to be rapidly dissolving in the downpour.

She tried to ignore the happy sot who was eyeing her at the moment. He belched his appreciation before thrusting his thumbs behind the lapels of a threadbare red coat that had once belonged to an officer, and staggered off.

Madame shrugged. "You have not enough experience. But I have need of an assistant who speaks English like a lady and French as well. Perhaps you will do. Come with me."

"Yes! *Bien sur!* Of course! *Certainement!* But I cannot walk!"

Isabelle looked down. Madame's little dog, which had been observing her as carefully as his mistress, had wound his lead around her ankles by way of introducing himself. He barked enthusiastically.

"Fig—*silence.*" But Madame seemed pleased when Isabelle reached down to stroke the dog's ears, not minding a bit that he had muddied her dress even more. Isabelle was quite fond of dogs, no matter what the weather.

"Hello, Fig!"

The dog barked again, at Madame this time, giving his mistress a look that was very like a smile.

"Ah. He likes you. It is a good sign. Fig is an intelligent animal."

She tugged the little dog's lead and walked around Isabelle twice to free the girl's ankles, then took her arm.

"*Merci,* Madame," Isabelle said, suddenly wondering where they might be going. In another moment, Madame steered her to the left down a different avenue as they continued their odd conversation, and then directed her to the right, into Clarges Street.

"Here." Madame Zazou carefully folded her umbrella and pointed up a flight of stairs to a three-story house of white stone. "Go in. I shall have someone bring you dry clothes." She looked Isabelle up and down, as if taking her measure by eye. "*Très bien.* Very good. We are of a size, *chérie.*"

"Ah—I am most grateful for your assistance, Madame," Isabelle said nervously, hoping that she was not about to enter a house of ill repute. "But—"

"But what?" Madame asked serenely. "Then we will have coffee and brioche, and you will tell me the rest of your story."

Isabelle looked up, noting a ragged opening in the clouds and a glimpse of the morning sky behind it. At the very least, the strangest night of her life was now over and breakfast was imminent.

# CHAPTER 3

*In which we return to the present . . .*

"The pawn advances, Nigel." Jeremy Gresham
held the chess piece in midair before committing
to his move. "And it intends to become a queen—
just like our Miss Sharpe. Though I suppose she
would settle for becoming a countess." He set
down the pawn upon the chessboard with a deci-
sive thump, precisely where it would cause the
most trouble.

Nigel raked a hand through his hair and sighed.
He studied the board, looking for an advantage
and finding none. "I am ready to concede the
match, Jeremy." He suddenly longed to do something—anything—that did not require him to cud-
gel his brains.

"Very well." His opponent began to collect the
pieces, not seeming terribly disappointed. Nigel was
very good at chess and Jeremy seldom won. "Perhaps
I should not have mentioned Miss Sharpe."

"Oh no—she is of no importance. It is just that the day is uncommonly fine and I had hoped to ride in Hyde Park before sunset."

Jeremy looked at him narrowly. "Piffle. You were losing, Nigel. Not like you. Not like you at all."

Nigel shrugged. "One cannot always win."

"You could have easily halted my advance, you know." Jeremy took a few pieces from his cupped hand and set them back on the board to make his point. "Like this—"

Damn the man. Was there anything more annoying than accepting defeat with good grace—and then being told how he might have triumphed? He scowled ferociously at his friend and swept the chessmen to the floor. "Just tell me how to stop Miss Sharpe, if you please!"

Jeremy bent down to pick them up. "Aha—I thought as much."

Nigel crossed his arms over his broad chest and leaned perilously far back in his chair.

"You are on the verge of disaster," Jeremy hastened to point out.

"I am in no danger," said Nigel. "But my uncle is."

"I meant the chair," Jeremy sighed. "But do go on."

"As you have guessed, Miss Phoebe Sharpe is on my mind. I said nothing against her at first. Truly, it did not concern me overmuch and my uncle is a notorious chaser of petticoats. But this seems to be no passing fancy."

The other man put the chess pieces into the neatly fitted drawer under the inlaid chess table and closed it. It was the only uncluttered surface in his drawing room, as Jeremy, a writer and publisher, covered every flat space with books and manuscripts.

"I must agree. The fair Phoebe has redoubled her efforts to ensnare your dear old uncle, now that the season is ending."

Nigel nodded. "Her gowns are cut lower than ever, and she is forever fanning herself so as to draw attention to her remarkable bosom, complaining of the heat."

Jeremy laughed, rather rudely.

Nigel shot him a worried look. "No one can wield a fan like Phoebe. It is a dangerous weapon in her pretty hands."

"They do not call her the Vixen of Vauxhall for no reason. But surely your uncle cannot be so easily beguiled. Was he not once known as the Lecher of Piccadilly?"

"Indeed not!"

Jeremy rose and paced the cluttered room, knocking assorted papers and a dictionary to the floor without seeming to care. Brilliant if not wellborn— and entirely self-educated, as far as Nigel knew—the man probably owned more books than anyone in London.

He spoke at last. "The earl is a worldly man, Nigel, and he must know that Phoebe may not be as innocent as she seems. I myself have seen her at Almack's whispering in corners with one fellow or another."

"But Bertie has not. I fear he is in for an unpleasant surprise. However, she has not done anything that would break his old heart—yet. He is not in the best of health these days."

His friend nodded agreement. "The earl is a constant visitor to the apothecary."

"Is there any tittle-tattle that you do not know, Jem?"

Jeremy smiled broadly. "Gossip is my bread-and-butter. How would I fill up the columns of my news sheets if I did not obtain such useful information? I might have to invent it all and that is far too much work."

Nigel threw up his hands. "Well, I cannot lie and tell Bertie that his little dove, as he calls her, has been unfaithful—for she has not."

"You have only to wait for her to make some misstep, then go to him straightaway."

Nigel shook his head. "He might forgive her. I believe he loves her in his fashion and I know that he has obtained a special license. They can marry when and where they wish."

"Interesting. And you mentioned a wager before we began our game. What of that?"

"Some damned fool has just entered it in the book at White's," Nigel said gloomily. "Probably Sheridan. A small fortune has been staked."

Jeremy's bright blue eyes gleamed with merriment. "Ah, yes. Now I remember. It involved Madame's Zazou's famous Invisible Arrangement. Now, if it can be proved that Phoebe's glorious bosom owes much to artifice—"

Irked by the other man's enjoyment of this ticklish situation, Nigel would not let him finish. "Hearing of his darling's public humiliation will infuriate Bertie! He will feel compelled to defend her honor, such as it is, with pistols at dawn."

Jeremy nodded. An understanding of what was at risk fought with his love of scandal—and understanding won. "I see. The earl is too old to fight duels, let alone arise before the sun. His hands will shake from the excitement and he will miss—but the other fellow may not."

"Precisely."

Jeremy seemed to be deep in thought. At last he spoke. "The matter is simple enough. To protect your uncle, you must protect Phoebe."

"How?"

"First you must gain the confidence of Madame Zazou, the inventress of the Invisible Arrangement—my sweet Mrs. Baddeley owns several. The uplifting effect is quite astonishing, I assure you."

"And does Mr. Baddeley experience the same astonishment at the sight of such beauty bare? By the way, was there ever an actual person of that name or did Grace invent him?"

"Do you know, I have never asked her," Jeremy said thoughtfully. "Perhaps Mr. Baddeley was eaten by a crocodile."

"I see."

"Well—never mind. As I said, you must make the acquaintance of Madame Zazou and proceed from there," Jeremy said. "I stand ready to offer excellent advice and whatever intelligence I can glean from my own sources, of course."

Nigel was exasperated beyond measure, and his voice betrayed it. "So I am to hobnob with a staymaker, is that it?"

"Yes—if you wish Madame Zazou to keep Phoebe's secret."

"That cannot be her real name. Is she even French?"

"I believe it is an alias, but she is most certainly

French. Grace has conversed with her most graciously in that language."

"But I cannot. My French is far from fluent," Nigel pointed out.

"Madame also speaks English. She has been in this country for some time. She fled the Terror in France some years ago and conceals her identity to protect herself and her aged mother."

"A likely story."

"Whether or not you believe it, you will have to become her friend."

Nigel scowled. "However, Madame may not have fitted Phoebe for an Invisible Arrangement. So nothing has been proved one way or another."

"Her establishment produces all manner of underpinnings," Jeremy said cheerfully. "Grace has got a lovely pair of lace drawers—dash it, inspiration strikes! And I cannot find anything to write with! My quill, where is my quill?"

He rummaged atop his desk for a pen, found one, found the inkwell and nearly knocked it over, then turned over a scribbled-upon piece of foolscap to jot a few lines on the back. He straightened and struck an orator's pose, clearing his throat before reading from the paper.

"*O, to lie in bed with Grace—wearing drawers made of lace*—how do you like it so far?"

"Needs work," Nigel said dryly. "It is not clear which one of you is wearing the lace drawers."

His friend rolled up the foolscap and rapped him on the head with it. "I am, of course!" he joked.

"If you would stick to the question, I would be much obliged."

Jeremy crossed the room to the pier glass and admired his reflection, smoothing down the few wisps of hair that remained upon his pate. He was short and remarkably ugly, but a great favorite of society women, who adored his endless supply of gossip.

"What was the question, Nigel?"

Nigel observed his preening friend with amusement. "I have not asked it yet. Madame Zazou was once pointed out to me, so I know what she looks like. But not where she lives."

Jeremy laughed in his good-natured way. "I can tell you that and whatever else that you require. I know all sorts of things about all sorts of people."

"And I have no doubt that many regret ever making your acquaintance."

"They fascinate me, Nigel—and their stories are better than anything I can make up. I owe my extraordinary success to the foolishness of others." He waved one hand with a grand flourish, as if acknowledging an unseen audience.

"Do not give yourself airs, Jem. You started out as a Grub Street hack."

The other man grinned with satisfaction. "And now I am a rich hack, with an interesting new sideline—some pay me handsomely not to mention them at all. The only thing more lucrative than a scandal is suppressing one, fortunately for me. Newspapers and novels are a penny-a-line business."

"At least you are honest. I suppose that counts for something."

Jeremy dismissed the cynical remark with a snort. "The fashionable world is what it is, Nigel. But you have avoided scandal thus far, though you are much admired by the ladies of the town, according to Grace—"

Nigel merely shrugged. "I do not make my affairs public."

Jeremy studied him for a moment. "You have told me nothing of them, as usual. Are you currently between amours, my friend?"

"I am. Not that it is any of your business."

Jeremy ignored this. "I know a woman—"

"No, thank you. You know too many women."

"Dear me. Has our dashing Nigel taken a vow of celibacy? I wonder how long that will last."

Nigel sighed. "I must resolve this matter of Phoebe and my uncle before I rejoin the amorous fray. Though to tell the truth, I have grown weary of the game—"

Jeremy slid his arms into the sleeves of his frock coat, preparing for his daily stroll from Paternoster Row to the pie-woman's shop. There he would purchase a meat pasty to keep up his strength before walking along Fleet Street to that teeming thoroughfare, the Strand. This ritual never varied and Nigel had never known his friend to miss it, no matter what the weather.

"Never! Can it be true?" Jeremy asked with mock astonishment. "The brave, the bold, the brilliant Nigel Wollaston—about to be leg-shackled? And who is the winsome miss, if I may ask?"

Nigel handed the other man his hat with a sigh. "There is no one, Jeremy—and I only said I was weary of the game. I went with Sheridan and Browne and the others to Vauxhall the other night, and was not even tempted to speak to the jades I saw, let alone trifle with them in the lanes."

That was not entirely true. There had been one lovely miss, shy and sweet, dressed in some soft color he could not quite make out in the half-light. She had dropped her fan, which he returned to her. He still remembered her musical voice and her quiet words of thanks.

Their encounter was accidental and the dropped fan was not a flirtatious ruse—his friends had pointed out the mysterious Madame Zazou, devouring sweets with an elderly male companion, and the girl had been by chance not far away.

Though unaccompanied, she was clearly gently bred and undoubtedly separated from her companions for only a moment. She and Nigel had gone their separate ways quickly enough.

Jeremy interrupted his thoughts. "If a man is tired of London, he is tired of life, or so they say. Your indifference is alarming. Are you quite well, Nigel?"

"Of course. Fit as a fiddle, though why a fiddle is considered fit is something I cannot fathom." Nigel gave his friend a hearty slap on the back. "Now, Jem, if you dare to put one word of this conversation in print, even with the unsubtle dashes and tantalizing initials you employ—*the distinguished Mr. G—— has heard that Lord W—— has said,* et cetera—I shall thrash you thoroughly and then sue you for libel."

Jeremy looked pained. "Nigel, you are my oldest friend. I have never so much as alluded to you or your family in print or anywhere else."

"That is true."

The other man waved his quill. "And now—would you like Madame Zazou's address?"

"Yes. Thank you, Jeremy."

Jeremy jotted it down. "Madame might not welcome your inquiries. She is famously discreet. You might try flirting with her assistant first."

Nigel groaned. "So I am to sink even lower and dally with the staymaker's assistant, is that it? No doubt she is a horrid old camel who loathes men and dips snuff. What if she spits? What if she turns me away? What if—?"

"Do not assume the worst," Jeremy said with a twinkle. "I hear that Madame's assistant is young and quite charming. But I knows nothing else about her besides her name."

"Which is?"

"Miss Isabelle Mousey."

# CHAPTER 4

*And we return to the lady in question . . .*

That same afternoon, Isabelle sat down by the sunny, second-floor window of the house in Clarges Street, next to a large sewing box that stood open—indeed, it would not close, overflowing as it was with ribbons, embroidery silk, and scraps in an untidy riot of colors.

She had work to do but chose to spend a few minutes thinking over how strange a turn her life had taken—and how odd it was to be taken for a servant by people of her own class.

For example, the fashionables taking the late-afternoon air upon the pavement below seemed not to see her behind the glass, but Isabelle cared not a whit.

She preferred not to be noticed, for many reasons. Living in London—unchaperoned and incognito—was a very great pleasure.

She was enjoying her unexpected adventure immensely. As Madame's assistant, she could come and go in a way that Lady Griselda never would have permitted.

Grateful to be away from her great-aunt's dreary parade of young curates, Isabelle seldom thought of the Priory and her sheltered life there. And marrying—let alone marrying well—was the last thing on her mind.

However, Madame had warned her rather pointedly that London provided no end of opportunity for romantic encounters, and the streets were full of strolling couples, now that it was spring. But Isabelle had met only one man thus far, quite unexpectedly. A handsome fellow, strolling the Vauxhall lanes with his friends, had picked up the fan she had dropped. The memory of that accidental encounter was oddly sweet.

For the moment she would just as soon remain invisible to men and everyone else. Lady Griselda never came to London, but Isabelle took every possible precaution not to be recognized—what if an acquaintance of her aunt's should chance to walk by upon some crowded street and remember Isabelle's face?

She concealed her hair under wide-brimmed bonnets and dressed modestly, preferring to see and not to be seen as far as she could contrive to do so.

The thought of returning to the Priory made her shudder. But by great good luck, she had stumbled upon a way to send an occasional letter there.

Isabelle had met James, the old footman, quite by chance at the Covent Garden market less than a week after she had arrived in London. She had been as surprised to see him as he was to see her.

He had come to the city upon a mission of utmost importance, which he had accomplished: Mrs. Pursley had sent him to London with the turtle and strict instructions to release it into the Thames on an outgoing tide.

"I dragged it from under the briers, miss, and put it into a basket. 'Twere a narrow escape from the soup for the poor beast, but Mrs. Pursley insisted. She promised me a pudding of me own come Christmas, with hextra raisins. I am fond of raisins, miss."

"Yes, James."

"So I put it into the river and hoped it might live. I did the best I could. But do not tell Lady Griselda of it, for the turtle cost her a pretty penny, you may be sure."

Isabelle wondered what had happened when Griselda discovered that it had gone missing, but James, garrulous to a fault, explained that straightaway before she asked.

"Mrs. Pursley made a mock turtle soup in an old shell, with cream and mushrooms. And mind you, her ladyship and that fool of a vicar did not know the difference. But it is a secret, of course."

Isabelle nodded, much amused by his tale. "And now you must keep a secret for me. Do not inform Lady Griselda of my exact whereabouts, for she assumes I reside with the duke—"

James had looked at her narrowly. "But where do you reside, miss?"

He had accepted her long and not entirely truthful explanation in due course and agreed to carry letters between her and Lady Griselda upon his occasional forays to London.

They settled upon a regular meeting place and

time, and, most important, he promised to tell Mrs. Pursley that Isabelle was safe and well.

The loyal cook would never give away her whereabouts, Isabelle knew.

She gleaned details from *The Tatler* and similar publications to enliven her weekly missive to Griselda, leaving out the scurrilous gossip about noble personages and their ignoble scandals, but describing at length the gowns, the entertainments, and the gallant gentlemen and sweet ladies with fluttering fans. And she always added a hasty postscript: dear Oswald sends warm regards and remains very truly yours, etc.

Fortunately, Lady Griselda never replied.

Isabelle had slipped the first coins she earned into the hand of the caretaker of the duke's house, bidding him to hold any post that might be addressed to her. The old man—the very fellow who had told her that the duke was dead upon the night she had arrived—had cackled happily over this unexpected remuneration, but his answer each week was the same: there was no letter for Miss Mousey.

So she met James on alternate Thursdays, at a flower-seller's stall, and gave him two letters—one for Lady Griselda and one for Mrs. Pursley. The latter included all the scurrilous gossip but left out the warm regards of the dead duke. She reassured the cook over and over that she had not gone on the town, taken a lover, or in any other way compromised her reputation, but was among friends, having the time of her life before she returned to the country once more.

When not busy in the house or helping Madame with her accounts—she was very good at sums and had soon cleared up some troubling discrepancies—Isabelle wandered where she pleased during the day. She was usually accompanied by Robert, the golden-haired page who was rather a pet of the women in the house, on one errand or another.

Her drab dresses enabled her to walk unnoticed, enjoying the hubbub of the busy streets as she looked for sundry items in shades that Madame did not already have upon her shelves.

And on days when the carriage was free, she sometimes persuaded Alf, the coachman, to drive her and Robert all the way to the booksellers along the Strand (it was here that she bought the newspapers and scandal sheets she needed for her letters home) or further on to the Smithfield market.

Robert relished these outings—he was devoted to Miss Mousey, who treated him with the loving kindness of an affectionate older sister, and the basket he carried for her never seemed heavy to him.

Heading north from the house, they would walk through Mayfair to the mercer's shop on Old Bond Street, looking through the windows at the glorious array of fine silks and velvets, and from there to the draper's for linen, and finally ending at the haberdasher's for ribbons and trim and other small items.

Robert, who was ten and never, ever tired, would beg to double back all the way to Hyde Park, where he could skip stones over the glassy surface of the Serpentine. There Miss Mousey might sit upon a bench and discreetly observe the riders on Rotten Row and the elegant women who promenaded nearby.

Her careful observations of changing fashions in dress—a frill here and a fichu there—were reported later to Madame Zazou, who noted these details for future reference.

Isabelle looked out the window, delaying her work a few moments longer, recollecting how pleasant the morning had been. The day had dawned clear and the sky had soon lightened to a springlike pale blue, with fleecy white clouds sailing overhead.

Their shopping expedition had taken longer than expected and Robert was swinging the basket with perilous abandon when Isabelle announced that their errands were done and turned in the direction of home.

"Robert, if you look inside, you will find a ginger-cake."

He gave her a gap-toothed grin. "When did you buy that, miss?"

"While you were feeding the apple core to the drayhorse, and petting his nose, and inquiring of his master as to the cost of oats and hay."

"I should like to own a horse and waggon of my own someday. Then I could sit up on the box, grand as you please in a top hat, like Alf. I would take you anywhere you wanted to go." He searched under the small parcels in the basket and found the cake. "You are very kind to think of me. We would make a fine show."

She patted his head as he looked up at her, his eyes full of daydreams that she hoped would come true. Like her, the boy was an orphan, with no one to look out for him.

He took a large bite, despite her reproving look. "It is delishuous," he mumbled through the crumbs.

"Do not gobble your food, Robert. It will trouble your stomach."

"Nothing troubles me when I am with you, Miss Mousey." He stretched up on his toes to give her an impulsive, spice-scented kiss upon the cheek.

Of such small pleasures were Isabelle's days composed—and she knew she would miss Robert, and Madame, who had become a dear friend indeed, when the time came for her to return to the Priory. She put that thought from her mind and set to work.

# CHAPTER 5

*Where paths cross again . . .*

Madame desperately needed Isabelle's assistance. The exquisites were clamoring in ever greater numbers for Invisible Arrangements, and Madame's seamstresses were hard put to fill the orders. She had trained them all well, but no one could sew all day and all night.

From their tête-à-têtes over coffee, Isabelle knew that the Frenchwoman's London success had been won at a price. Once Madame had been the most sought-after corsetière in Paris—before the Terror and its howling minions had removed the heads of most of her clientele.

In the years since she had established herself here, fashions changed and artless, high-waisted dresses came into vogue. The Frenchwoman's uncommon skill at making small things bigger and big things smaller made her much in demand.

It was said that every fashionable beauty of the

present day owed her success to the Invisible Arrangement. It was one of these that Isabelle was attempting to sew now, though she was rather better at embroidery than plain seams.

She studied Madame's hastily scribbled instructions once more and set her pincushion on the paper to hold it flat. Then she crossed one knee over the other in a rather unladylike way and began to join two pieces of material.

Two minutes later, she looked down and muttered a word that Madame Zazou used occasionally. It was not a word Isabelle would ever say in English, but it sounded better in French.

She had absentmindedly sewn the delicate cloth in her lap to her own dress and would have to snip out the tiny stitches and start over. She scrabbled through the sewing box for a pair of small scissors. *Snip. Snip. Snip.* The painstaking task made her squint. At least Madame Zazou was not here to remark upon Isabelle's clumsiness. *Snip. Snip.* She had to be careful not to snip a hole in her own dress—it was her best, a gray silk handed down from Madame—or the nearly transparent linen that went into each Invisible Arrangement.

The thing could not be seen under the bodice of the sheerest dress once dampened with water, but it supported female flesh in a most astonishing way.

Isabelle had tried one on, marveling at the splendid rise of her bosom. The effect was created by careful fitting, which Madame did personally for each customer, though she left the actual construction to her well-trained seamstresses.

Invisible Arrangements were cheap to make and quick to sew, considering that they amounted to no more than a few scraps of material. The simplicity of Grecian-style costume did not require complicated stays or busks.

Such elaborate constraints had gone the way of hooped skirts, panniers, and powdered hair. Isabelle suddenly thought of a Priory portrait of young Lady Griselda sporting a bizarre coiffure high enough to conceal an owl, her ample bosom squeezed and flattened by an old-fashioned corset.

Madame's wonderful invention did twice the work of these for a fraction of the cost, and the clients who flocked in asked to have dressmaking done as well.

But the Invisible Arrangement was her most profitable item. A young seamstress, since sacked for her talkativeness, had revealed the secret of its construction on Isabelle's first day as Madame's assistant.

"Plump ladies is wrapped in linen, like high-gyptian mummies. Some pops out the top—it is funny to see them stuff it back in. But thin ladies need padding inside their Hinvisible Harrangements. Not that you need one, miss. Your figure is perfect. Like the naughty wench on that old jug there."

The girl had pointed to one of Madame's Grecian vases, which were proudly displayed on a wide shelf—high-gyptian mummies, Roman statuary, and the glory that was Greece being the height of fashion.

Every great house boasted many such objects, with the understandable exception of the mummies, which sensible people gave to the British Museum.

Vases like Madame's, adorned with gods and god-

desses prancing about rather tipsily and disporting
themselves in shocking ways, were very popular.
These happy deities wore abbreviated tablecloths
when they wore anything at all, and elegant females imitated them shamelessly.

A venerable admirer had given Madame her
vases—and he had also deeded her the town house
on Clarges Street and provided capital for her fledg-
ling business a few years ago, along with a generous annuity.

Madame always spoke of the fellow with great affection, though he was no longer alive. In fact,
overcome by the demonstrative force of her grati-
tude, he had conveniently expired in her bed. The
sight of Madame's flawless form in a diaphanous
costume of her own design had been the *coup de
grace.*

Or so said the women of the house. Isabelle was
inclined to believe them.

There—she had cut the piece of linen free at last
and proceeded to pin it properly before resuming
her sewing. She studied the instructions again, admiring Madame's handwriting, which was elegant
even when she wrote in haste.

No matter what, Madame strove for perfection,
even if she rarely held others to such exacting stan-
dards.

She was forgiving by nature, though fate had not
always been kind to her. Throughout her many adventures, beginning with her escape from blood-
thirsty revolutionaries who hoped to make her pay
for the sins of her aristocratic customers, she had
sided with the common folk, not being nobly born
herself. But she'd had no wish to be a martyr to

their cause, and the mobs were not known for listening to reason.

Hiding by day and traveling by night, she had managed to save her own life and that of her mother, a lacemaker, blind like so many in her profession. But Madame's younger sister—she told Isabelle, with tears in her eyes, how much she resembled this unfortunate girl—had died of fever en route.

Madame's mother lived upon the top floor, where the gentle old lady could hear the birds she loved and grow herbs and scented geraniums in window boxes. Jehane had her own lady's-maid and wanted for nothing.

Isabelle had grown quite fond of her, having no mother of her own. Jehane was much loved and respected by all in the house but addressed by her first name, at her request, and never Zazou.

Madame had explained with a demure smile that they had been helped by the Zazous, a troupe of acrobats, during their perilous journey out of France. She had needed an alias and the name had stuck, being easy to remember, despite her mother's disapproval.

Isabelle had no idea what their real family name was and did not ask. If Madame was kind enough not to pry into her background—and she never did—Isabelle would return the favor.

Wishing not to be a burden, Jehane industriously plied her pins and bobbins, using her skilled sense of touch to create the lace designs she had learned in a convent workshop as a child, when she still had her sight.

Madame Zazou sold every piece to older women who still wore lace, but this fragile finery was no longer as valuable or as fashionable as it once had been. Isabelle sometimes overheard bits of their whispered conversations and knew that Jehane sent the money she made to relatives in France, with her daughter's help and blessing.

For these reasons and others, no one had a right to judge the morals of Madame, in Isabelle's decided opinion, though the older woman admittedly displayed a Frenchwoman's practicality when it came to romance. If she occasionally received financial assistance or other favors from a gentleman or two, that was Madame's own affair.

But it was one more reason for Isabelle to stay far away from Lady Griselda for as long as possible. If Griselda knew of Madame's profession or her principles—or that Isabelle had impulsively decided to live in a most unusual sort of household—she would undoubtedly fly into a fury. The thought made Isabelle smile again.

She set aside her fine sewing for the moment and turned to another project, threading a narrow ribbon through the edge of a delicate chemise sheer enough to see through. This would be worn over an Invisible Arrangement and an equally sheer dress would be worn over both. Its wearer would appear to be nearly nude.

She cast her eyes down at her own serviceable gray silk gown. Though it was eminently respectable, she hated it with a passion, mostly because she was tired of wearing it. Her meager salary did not permit the extravagance of new clothes—but gray was a good color not to be noticed in.

A rustle and a thump made her turn, and she rose to pick up a bolt of costly fabric that had slipped from a high shelf to the floor, sighing over its beauty.

The shelves were crowded with delicate stuffs suitable for the approaching summer: muslins, delicate calicoes, and embroidered white mull from faraway India.

Temptation surrounded her, spilling forth in an infinite variety of subtle colors and textures. Isabelle's imaginary wardrobe included a dress in each fabric, with gloves, shawls, bonnets, and shoes of every description.

Her real wardrobe included—very little. But as she had decided not to be noticed, it scarcely mattered. It was oddly exhilarating not to worry about such things.

*Clink.* Had a pebble hit the window? Who had thrown it?

She rose and looked out. An uncommonly handsome man, strongly built and tall, with very dark hair, was gazing up at her and smiling.

Unthinkingly, she touched a hand to her heart as if to say—*me?*

He nodded, just as though she had spoken. His face was familiar, his dark eyes compelling even from this distance. But where had she seen him before?

*Vauxhall . . . and only a week ago.*

Yes, that was it. He was the very fellow who had returned her fan that night. Isabelle smiled in return, a little surprised by her own forwardness. But seeing him made her heart flutter—a delightful sensation and one she had never experienced until the first time they had met. The memory came back to her with a rush of feeling she did not quite comprehend. . . .

\* \* \*

*Lisa Noeli*

The excursion to Vauxhall had been proposed by Madame, who wanted to show the pleasure garden by the Thames to Isabelle—suitably chaperoned, of course. It occurred to Isabelle that the older woman watched over her carefully, and sometimes she wondered why. Madame herself was to be accompanied by yet another venerable admirer.

The older woman seemed to attract them with astonishing ease and Isabelle simply assigned the initials V.A. to each, to save the trouble of remembering names.

The clamor and the crowds, and, finally, the fireworks, had given Isabelle a prodigious headache. Trailing behind, wanting no more than a glass of cold water and a quiet place to sit, though neither were to be had, she fanned herself vigorously—until the fan, a contrived affair of plumy feathers from Madame's discarded stock, slipped from her damp hand.

At that moment, the tallest of a group of boisterous fellows turned away from his friends to assist her, picking up the fan and proffering it with a gentlemanly flourish.

She took it, touching his hand by accident for a fraction of a second, not knowing exactly what to say or do and feeling very awkward. She was unaccompanied, strictly speaking. Madame and the V.A. had strolled ahead to purchase a paper cone of sweetmeats. Perhaps this fellow thought she dropped the fan on purpose to capture his attention, but nothing could be further from the truth.

Isabelle hoped he would not think she was one of the many young women of dubious reputation who accosted men in the dark and winding lanes.

She thanked him quickly and hastened away, trying to catch up to Madame.

But she glanced back. The tall gentleman was observing her thoughtfully, a half-smile playing about his lips.

The group of men began to talk once more, though much more quietly, studying Madame as they did so. Isabelle wondered why.

She turned her head and saw the older woman licking a trace of powdered sugar from a fingertip. *Most* unladylike. But Madame Zazou adored sweets, all manner of sweets, with an unholy passion. Surely her minor lapse of manners did not call for so steady a scrutiny or so much whispered discussion.

Madame seemed not to notice that anyone was watching, indifferent as always to the opinions of others. Isabelle decided to follow suit, casting one last look at the gentleman and his friends. They wandered off in the direction of the supper boxes, no doubt wanting to refresh themselves with the infamous and devilishly intoxicating punch.


She had thought infrequently of the man from Vauxhall since—but now, only one week later, here he was. He seemed delighted beyond measure to see her. Had he followed them home that night or found out through other means where she lived?

He was gazing at her with extraordinary intensity, as if there was something he wanted, something only she could give—Isabelle told herself firmly not to be so silly.

He was simply looking at her and that was all.

Surely the fellow was not suddenly moonstruck

simply because he had happened to see her. No, that was impossible, plainly dressed as she was in gray, her hair pinned up hastily, with a few escaped curls to bedevil her.

But he would not move on. He was handsome. And very dashing, although soberly dressed. Such a man could talk anyone into opening the door and bound up the stairs to her in the wink of an eye. And Isabelle *was* alone, at least in this room, though others were about somewhere within the enormous house.

An impromptu flirtation would be most improper, even if the thought made her heart soar with happiness. Nonetheless, she put on a stern face—but he gave her a wide, boyish grin in response.

Isabelle was undone. Once more, she smiled back.

# CHAPTER 6

*Introducing a most important person . . .*

Nigel was delighted. To have been granted such fetching smiles, of such disarming sweetness, was an unexpected pleasure indeed.

So the charming girl he had seen at Vauxhall was Madame Zazou's assistant—what extraordinary good luck and what a delightful surprise.

He knew that the members of White's would be equally delighted to make her acquaintance for underhanded reasons of their own. Miss Isabelle Mousey might—or might not—know things the fools would love to learn.

Thanks goodness he had confided in Jeremy. He had found out Miss Mousey's name—and confirmed that Miss Sharpe's inexpressibles were indeed made by the seamstresses of Madame Zazou's establishment. Nigel was deeply grateful. He silently vowed to buy several copies of Jeremy's next book.

But before he did anything idiotic, like serenade the beauty at the window, he reminded himself why he had come.

Reason One: his uncle was falling in love with Phoebe. But hang it all, what the trollop wore or didn't wear under her shockingly low-cut gowns was her own concern and Bertie was not likely to care.

Reason Two: the earl would not be pleased if his beloved were to become a laughingstock and might feel compelled to defend her honor. This impossible task would undoubtedly shatter his fragile health.

Nigel then reminded himself of his plan to bribe everyone in this house, from Madame Zazou to the least of the seamstresses, to keep Phoebe's secret—if there was a secret to keep.

One question remained: how was he to gain entry to this *sanctum sanctorum* of feminine charm?

The answer was smiling down upon him.

The beautiful Miss Mousey was bound to leave the house upon some errand sooner or later.

He gazed up at Isabelle. She was even more enchanting than he remembered, all the more so for her modest gray dress. Her brown eyes shone with merriment and intelligence, her features quite perfect, and her hair was the color of golden honey. She was no more than twenty, by his guess.

Her rosy-pink lips, parted ever so slightly when she smiled, were ripe for kissing—had she ever been kissed?

He would love to be the first to do so.

Her graceful demeanor and cultured tone of voice had impressed him most favorably at Vauxhall, though she had spoken but a few words to him on that night.

He longed to hear her voice again.

Miss Mousey simply gazed at him, *still* smiling—and was that a small dimple in her pretty cheek? Nigel could not be sure.

Once again, he fought an irrational urge to burst into song like a lovesick lad in an operetta. However, unlike the sets of Drury Lane theatres, the town house had no trellis or other convenient structure to climb and warble in a fluty tenor of his feelings for his dearest love, his little dove, tra-la and so on.

His voice was just below a baritone, in any case, with a faint growl in it on days that followed nights of revelry. And try as he might, he never sang on key. The lady was not likely to listen to any serenade he might offer for long. But she did not move away from the window, almost as if she were waiting to see what he would do next.

He considered the likelihood that Madame Zazou's houseman, a grizzled brute of alarming size whom he had glimpsed at the door, would send him sprawling into the street if he were to venture up the stairs with the hope of gaining entry. Madame's customers were exclusively female, as far as Nigel knew.

His thoughts were interrupted by the clatter of a carriage rattling by, which came to a clamorous halt several yards ahead.

A footman in gorgeous new livery bristling with buttons jumped out and offered his hand to a young lady—oh, no. Not *that* young lady. Not Miss Phoebe Sharpe herself. Nigel's luck had suddenly turned and not for the better.

Had she seen him? Well, she would, and within a second or two. Nigel could not simply run for it but he did wish the earth would simply swallow him up and spit him out somewhere in the vicinity of his club.

Assisted by her footman, Phoebe alighted with a spring in her step. Everything about her seemed to quiver slightly, from her assiduously crimped curls to her overflowing bosom. This subtle and constant motion was what had caught his uncle's eye—and held the old man spellbound. It *was* an impressive sight, Nigel thought distractedly.

Miss Sharpe jiggled and quivered even more as she stepped daintily over the cobblestones, her pale curls shining in the afternoon sunlight and her flawless teeth displayed in a somewhat predatory smile—until she caught sight of Nigel.

Her eyes flashed and she gave him a fierce look. Nigel bowed ever so slightly to the woman who might be his aunt someday, knowing nothing of what was going through her mind at that moment.

"Good afternoon, Miss Sharpe."

She did not reply but busied herself with whatever needed fetching from the carriage, fuming silently.

What was *he* doing here? Oho—she could guess. Phoebe wanted to kick him. She had heard that he did not like her and that Bertie's brother, Lord Charles Wollaston, Nigel's father, did not approve of her. Like father, like son—and now he was spying on her.

She had just been informed of the wager at White's regarding her personal dimensions. The stakes had risen astronomically high since certain of Nigel's companions had come in on the bet— George Sheridan, that wretched tosspot, and William Browne, that muttonhead.

Her ears were still burning, thanks to a friend of a friend who had been so good as to tattle, and she was furious. If Nigel hoped to dissuade the old earl from marrying her—well, he could not, and that was that. Phoebe was determined to speed the arrival of that nuptial day.

She supervised the footman, who was unloading several parcels from the carriage, tapping her foot impatiently and looking about the street—everywhere but at Nigel.

Money-grubbing sod. Heartless beast. Handsome devil—oh, where had *that* thought come from? She simply could not allow herself to be distracted by physical charm, when circumstances forced her to hate him.

Obviously Nigel hoped that his uncle would die unmarried and without issue, passing the title of earl and his immense fortune to his disagreeable brother, who might then leave it all to Nigel.

Then she would simply have to marry Lord Charles, Nigel's father, and it would serve both of them right.

Phoebe had been the first to wish her dearest Bertie long life at a recent celebration honoring his birthday, praying silently that she might share those golden years—and the gold itself—with him. Everything had been going quite smoothly, until that damned bet had been made by Nigel's odious friends. He was undoubtedly behind it. But why?

By her reckoning, Nigel most likely would never inherit a thing, not even a rusty suit of armor from the echoing Great Hall of the earl's gloomy country house. He had nothing to gain by opposing her, but she stood to lose a great deal—oh, she didn't want to think about it a second longer.

"Tomkyns! Make haste!" she said imperiously to the footman. "And do be careful!" He fumbled with the parcels—there were many—under her watchful eye. But Phoebe's thoughts were not really on him.

When she became the countess and *she would be a countess*—she glared at Nigel, who pretended to be listening to a sparrow's trill and was studiously avoiding her gaze—she would have Bertie's clanking collection of armor immediately thrown into the nearest river. And she intended to spend every penny she could upon herself.

The footman straightened up, his arms laden, and they proceeded to Madame Zazou's establishment. Phoebe's fine new shoes pinched but she walked with dignified slowness, her head high.

At least no one was observing this unexpected encounter.

Fie upon her cursed fate—someone was. From the corner of her eye, she caught a glimpse of a young woman in a gray dress at the window above. Phoebe had seen her in the shops, with that young boy who worked for Madame, but could not remember her name. At the moment, Phoebe was so distracted that she could barely remember her *own* name.

Nigel was watching her now. She refused to give him the idea that she found him intimidating.

To be a great lady—and to swan it around a great estate—was her most cherished ambition. It was too bad if Nigel Wollaston did not like that idea or her.

She sniffed and tossed her curls, acknowledging him with the merest nod.

"Good afternoon, Mr. Wollaston," she replied at last.

"Why, Miss Sharpe—this is an unexpected pleasure."

The man was insufferable. Phoebe stalked away, trailed by her servant.

Nigel glanced up at the window again. Miss Mousey had vanished, and he heard the faint but vigorous barking of a dog within the house.

Miss Sharpe ascended the steps and raised her lace-mittened hand to the knocker, pounding it with an unladylike strength that made her bosom quiver all the more. The footman beside her could not look away.

The grizzled fellow who guarded the door opened it with a sweeping bow and waved the two inside, staring at Nigel in a distinctly unfriendly way.

Perhaps if he were to simply ask for admittance—no, Nigel decided. Not yet.

He watched Phoebe pass through the portals of Madame Zazou's and waited a minute longer for the door to shut. He looked up again to the high window, hoping for one last smile from the vision of loveliness he had seen there—and was suddenly rewarded for his patience.

Isabelle Mousey had reappeared and was gesturing in a way that meant—what? He understood that she could not simply open the window and call down to him like a housemaid, but he was damned if he knew what she might want, or why she signaled to him—

She turned quickly to speak to someone within the room—it was Madame Zazou, who waved her away from the window and took her place.

Madame studied him for several moments, with a faint smile upon her lips. She was a handsome woman for her years, he reflected, and undoubtedly a shrewd one. But why was she looking at him and what was she thinking? Under her measuring gaze, Nigel felt as bashful as a schoolboy. He drew a breath of relief when she, too, moved away from the window.

A small dog with brown ears and a white face, perhaps the one he had heard before, popped up upon the windowsill. It barked ferociously, as if letting Nigel know he would be eaten at once if he dared to linger.

He silently wished the little guardian well and strolled down the street, planning to return as soon as possible. At the moment, he needed coffee— very strong coffee—and a little time to plan his next move.

# CHAPTER 7

*A most interesting question is asked . . .*

The afternoon sunlight slanted through the work-room, crowded with women coming and going, their arms laden with bolts of goods destined to become dresses for the fair and the plain alike.

Madame had been advised by Isabelle to add a modiste and mantua-makers to her staff, owing to the success of her invention, and had done so. Since Isabelle's fortuitous arrival at her house, she had had no end of customers and it seemed that everything they touched turned to gold.

Miss Phoebe Sharpe had ordered ten outfits in all and the final fittings were underway. It was a tedious process, and that young lady was anything but patient.

At least the earl, the girl's only lover from what Madame knew, paid her bills promptly. She heard Phoebe stamp her foot on the floor of the chamber above and sighed as she went over the accounts in the small study that adjoined the workroom.

She had hired two more seamstresses to handle the extra sewing only last week. They were nimble-fingered girls, cousins of a woman already on her staff and trustworthy enough, she supposed.

Thanks to a talkative *demimondaine* who had just left, Madame had found out that Miss Sharpe had become the subject of a wager. Someone would collect a small fortune if a certain question could be answered correctly, and indisputable proof given of that answer. Did the young lady wear an Invisible Arrangement—or not?

Having heard of the bet in detail less than an hour ago, Madame had not told anyone, not even Isabelle, in whom she confided much. Keeping secrets was much easier when no one knew of them—not that the bet was a secret anymore.

Any of her seamstresses might be persuaded to talk, though they only did the sewing—Madame saw to the fitting. Still, if sweet words did not work, she knew only too well that the musical chime of golden coins might do the trick.

Her informant had explained the terms of the bet: the winner had to show proof that Phoebe had been measured for an Invisible Arrangement. Since so many women wore them, simply producing one of these flimsy garments was not enough. No, it would have to be a page in Madame's handwriting—which would also have to be verified—that gave all the details of the transaction.

And it had to be produced within three days or the bet was off. So Phoebe had a chance to bag her game—that old roué Bertie Wollaston himself—

before anyone won. The members of White's were nothing if not sportsmanlike.

It was all very silly but it could cause a great deal of trouble. Madame propped her chin upon a hand and considered the matter. Her reputation for discretion was the cornerstone of her business—and there would be other wagers concerning other women, if she did not put a stop to this nonsense now.

She needed an ally. Perhaps the young man who had been looking up so adoringly at Isabelle a short while ago would help—she knew that he was Bertie's nephew, since the admirer who had taken her to Vauxhall had noted Nigel in passing and said as much.

His presence here evidently flustered Phoebe—Madame had discerned that just by looking over Isabelle's shoulder, though Miss Sharpe had not seen Madame.

Or perhaps Phoebe knew of the bet. Madame Zazou had been aghast to overhear a silly miss and her donkeyish companion loudly discussing the matter right in front of the house shortly before Phoebe's arrival.

Such titillating talk had a way of spreading almost at once in London, through every level of society, as if the very words were actually floating in the breezy air of spring.

Gossip—how she hated it. There was no avoiding it, however. And the Frenchwoman knew nearly all there was to know about her clients—most women gabbled like geese to their modistes and hairdressers.

They could not keep a secret but she kept

theirs—in a small notebook with covers of thin boxwood. In this, using a curious code of her own invention, she jotted down the measurements of her clients, the garments they had ordered, and any special requirements.

The notebook was kept in a locked drawer of her tall desk, and the notebook also locked, by means of an ingenious, tiny mechanism. Madame set the account books aside and picked up both little keys with a thoughtful expression, stringing them upon a fine golden chain, ignoring the workaday hubbub in the next room.

She clasped the chain around her neck and tucked the little keys between her breasts where no one could see them. At the moment, Miss Phoebe Sharpe's exact dimensions were known to none but that young lady and herself, and she intended to keep it that way.

She could not let slip anything that might help the rogues at White's win that scandalous wager. Fools came and went, but customers were forever.

"Isabelle!" Madame called. "Please see to the charming customer upstairs—she is stamping her feet like a child." Madame apprised Isabelle quickly of Phoebe's needs and added some interesting details. "*Alors*, Miss Sharpe is a greedy little thing and the darling of an earl, as you know. I hope she can persuade him to spend a few hundred pounds upon her lingerie."

She rolled her eyes when she said this, adding a rude comment in French that made Isabelle laugh out loud. She ascended the stairs to the chamber above with a light heart. She had heard much concerning Miss Sharpe in the last weeks but but had always been out and about during her previous fittings.

Mrs. Violet Shrinking, a female dragon of advanced years, clad in rustling black bombazine, guarded the door of the fitting room. She spoke sharply to Robert as Isabelle reached the landing, startling her. "You there!"

The boy had made the mistake of glancing at the old lady on his way downstairs.

"Yes, Mrs. Shrinking?"

"None of your shifty looks, my lad! Be off!"

Robert gave her an angelic smile in return and kept his shins well away from Mrs. Shrinking's very large and pointed shoes as he proceeded about his household errands.

Once through the door, Isabelle tidied the room and arranged the folds of the heavy brocade draperies, though the rear window looked out onto the blank back wall of another house, and privacy was assured.

Madame entered soon enough and gave Miss Sharpe an inscrutable smile.

The young woman was perched prettily upon the chair that Madame called a bergère—a shepherdess chair. Isabelle suddenly imagined Phoebe painted in a rustic landscape, à la Watteau, with a crook and wide straw hat, tending to a flock of sheepish old men. The thought made her smile very politely indeed.

"Oh! I feel dreadfully faint," Phoebe said. "An unexpected encounter has upset my nerves. If one might have a glass of cordial, one would be most grateful."

She fanned herself vigorously as a seamstress

filled a small crystal glass with elderberry wine
from a decanter on a side table, not noticing
Madame's disapproving stare. Isabelle had a feeling that the Frenchwoman, who was otherwise
generous to a fault, would add the trifling expense
of this refreshment to Phoebe's bill.

"Imagine meeting Mr. Wollaston—dear Nigel—
right in front of your house, Madame. He is the
earl's nephew, you know, and a powerfully attractive man. But I might be his step-aunty soon.
Imagine *that!*" She giggled and drank the wine
rather noisily, draining the glass and holding it out
to be filled again.

Nigel Wollaston—so that was the name of the
dashing stranger. Isabelle had been quite unaware
that he had any connection to Phoebe, who had
scarcely looked in his direction when Isabelle was
watching them on the street below.

Such a connection seemed impossible—or perhaps Isabelle wanted it to be impossible. She
thought of the man from Vauxhall as *hers* somehow, though she knew the notion was irrational.

Her momentary dismay dissolved into amusement when she noticed Fig intently watching Miss
Sharpe. The little dog was curled up in his silk-
lined basket and bobbing his head like Phoebe's.

Hiding a smile, Isabelle reached down to pet
him but he jumped out of the basket as quickly as
he had jumped in, scratching at the door.

"He wishes to see Maman. Please let him out,
Isabelle," Madame said. Isabelle opened the door
to do so and noticed that Mrs. Shrinking was nod-
ding off. No matter. Old dragons might sleep
when and where they wished.

Phoebe drank her second glass of cordial as eagerly as the first. "Mr. Wollaston was pacing back and forth under the first floor window, Madame Zazou. Is he smitten with one of your girls?" She shot Isabelle a spiteful look over the rim of the little glass.

Madame frowned. "Certainly not."

"He is a powerfully attractive man," Phoebe repeated. "One might be tempted if one were not careful. One might be swept away."

"Indeed, Miss Sharpe." Isabelle said, politely enough. The undertone of this conversation was making her uneasy, and Phoebe seemed to be more than a little tipsy.

Phoebe continued. "But one cannot be swept away when one is on the verge of marriage," she said. "So one held one's—oh, grammar be damned—I held my head high and nodded to him most graciously. He is so concerned for his uncle Bertram—you know, the seventh earl of Skipwith, who has made no secret of his feelings for me. I am quite mad with longing for him, of course."

Isabelle caught Madame's look of disdain and what she said under her breath. *Petite vache.* Little cow. It was quite evident that Madame did not share Miss Sharpe's high opinion of herself.

"They are very close—one would think they were father and son. But that is not the case. Mr. Wollaston is merely his nephew, as I believe I mentioned. . . ." She prattled on, not making a great deal of sense after two glasses of wine.

Madame let her talk, wondering again if she knew of the wager at White's. But Phoebe made no mention of it, though Madame thought it unlikely that the gossip had not yet reached the younger woman's ears.

There was a soft knock upon the door and Madame opened it to let the modiste past the dragon.

Truth to tell, though Isabelle was grateful that Miss Sharpe had provided Nigel's name—there was no harm if she thought of him by his first name, surely—she found the chattering little goose otherwise most annoying as the afternoon wore on.

Phoebe exclaimed in a high-pitched voice over dress designs she liked and fluttered her dainty hands irritably at those she did not. The modiste was the soul of patience, unrolling more sketches of the latest fashions for Miss Sharpe's approval, murmuring assent whenever possible.

"So true, so true. In blue? I have in mind a certain shade of forget-me-not that would match your eyes to perfection. . . ."

The modiste opened a thick book of swatches that showed all the delicate hues of a summer garden in full bloom, silently hoping that the fussy little mademoiselle would make her choices without further ado.

Miss Sharpe frowned and waved the book away. "No. I do not like any. I must have. . . ."

She proceeded to describe the moonbeams-and-magic charm of a dress worn by her most elegant rival, down to the probable cost of the material, making a clever guess as to the manufacturer, an old firm in Spitalfields famous for its shot silk.

"Can it be bought today? My calendar is crowded and there is not much time—oh, the balls, fêtes, and galas to come! My head is buzzing! But everything must be in readiness!"

"As mademoiselle wishes," Madame said, somewhat frostily. She gestured to her lady's maid and instructed her in a whisper to summon Robert.

Isabelle knew she would be sent with him to actually make the purchase, and she was eager for an opportunity to leave the house. Miss Sharpe's pointed remarks had unsettled her.

Oh, it was impossible to believe that less than two hours ago she had been content to sit and sew—her world seemed to have turned upside down the moment she saw Mr. Wollaston.

She had been *so* tempted to call down to him—and had very nearly waved to him like a naïve girl fresh from the schoolroom, though she had turned away in time to stop herself.

At the very least she had checked her impulse to fling up the sash and ask him his name. Oddly, Madame, who had entered the room at that moment, had not scolded but only sent Isabelle away from the window to fetch a pair of scissors—and looked out herself.

How irksome to find that Miss Sharpe knew Nigel well. But if Phoebe had not come today, Isabelle might very well have gone down to the street, even exchanged a few words with him. So she supposed she had Phoebe to thank for something.

It occurred to Isabelle that her great-aunt would have called her a shameless hussy. Oh, well. Perhaps she was, but she did not particularly care. And Lady Griselda was many miles away in the Surrey countryside, inflicting her misguided and unwelcome charity upon one and all.

Isabelle turned her thoughts back to Nigel Wollaston. Just why he had lingered so long, like a lovesick swain, was something that still puzzled her. A gentleman—the nephew of an earl—would not, as a rule, so much as nod to a woman who seemed to be of a lower social class, even though they had met before.

Alas, she had been dressed no better than a governess, wearing rainy-day gray when the sun was out and the world was bright. But Nigel Wollaston had gazed up at her as if she were a very goddess, a most disconcerting experience.

She had liked it. Very much.

Isabelle sighed and turned her attention back to Miss Sharpe, who stood up somewhat unsteadily for her dress to be unfastened by Madame's young maid. The inexperienced girl undid the tiny buttons with care, one by one.

Miss Sharpe, quite pink in the face from the cordial, exhaled rather crossly and twisted her head round to see what was taking so long. The back seam ripped—and Miss Sharpe slapped the maid across the face.

Isabelle stepped forward to counter a second blow, should Phoebe slap the girl again, but Madame stopped her with an outstretched hand.

The Frenchwoman's dark eyes blazed with inner fire, as if she desired nothing more than to return the physical insult with all the strength she possessed. But she quietly dismissed the trembling maid, who fled the room in tears, and attended to Phoebe herself. "My apologies, Miss Sharpe," she said smoothly. "The torn seam can be mended while the fitting is done."

"Very well," Phoebe said haughtily. "But mind it does not happen again. I shall take my custom elsewhere."

Madame nodded without saying anything more

and pulled out a tall, black-lacquered screen, section by section. Isabelle had not seen this open before and she noted with interest the gold-painted scenes of simpering nymphs disrobing while satyrs looked on. How appropriate.

Phoebe marched behind the screen, followed by Madame, who helped her to undress. She handed out Miss Sharpe's clothes to Isabelle, who noted with annoyance that they smelled strongly of nervous sweat. For a second or two, she contemplated tossing them out the window . . . but surely there was a better, more lasting way to give Phoebe her comeuppance. Isabelle would think of it at her leisure.

She happened to glance out that window and her angry thoughts flew immediately from her mind.

What the devil? There *was* a devil, dangling from a rope against the blank rear wall of the house opposite. A roughly dressed man with coarse red hair kicked his hobnailed boots against the bricks to stay clear as an unseen confederate lowered him down. He gave a tug on the rope—which stopped in midair—and gave Isabelle an ugly grin.

She gasped, utterly shocked. Madame stepped out from behind the screen.

"*Attends*, Madame! *Regardez!*" She spoke in French and pointed, hoping Phoebe, who was still behind the screen, would not immediately comprehend her meaning.

Madame looked. The man grinned at her even more broadly, which caused a scar that ran from his jaw to his eyebrow to pull his expression into a lecherous smirk.

Without a doubt, someone had told the repulsive fellow of Phoebe's visit to her house—someone who knew that the fitting room was upstairs and in the back. But who? The question would have to be answered later. Madame pulled the hanging draperies swiftly together and plunged the room into near darkness.

"Oh, what now?" exclaimed Phoebe peevishly from behind the screen. Madame moved quickly to keep her there.

"*Zut*. A drapery is about to fall, mademoiselle! The support must be fixed—the rod is mahogany and quite heavy. We shall move to another chamber without windows or curtains. Isabelle, call for a manservant. Please, you must wear this robe—"

Phoebe emitted muffled squeaks as Madame, with a flick of her wrist, took a huge dressing gown from a nearby hook and turned its folds into a hood of sorts over the young woman's head.

Isabelle opened the door to allow some light in, waking Mrs. Shrinking, who gawked at the sight of Phoebe.

"Please come with me, Miss Sharpe—" Madame led her, complaining all the way, from the chamber and down the hall to another room.

Isabelle remained, moving the concealing drape ever so slightly to see if the intruder was still hanging against the opposite wall.

There he was, swinging like a monkey. Indeed, his red-brown hair and peculiar grimace made him look a perfect jackanapes.

What in heaven's name was going on?

# CHAPTER 8

*Behaving like barbarians . . .*

Madame rushed back into the darkened fitting room, gathering up Phoebe's clothes, fan, lace mittens, reticule—and the bottle of cordial. "Follow me. Pretend that nothing has happened."

Isabelle did as she was told, hurrying down the hall to a smaller room, where Miss Sharpe paced in the voluminous dressing gown. She tripped over it once but quickly regained her balance, glaring at both women and the numerous servants who had followed them into the room. "Am I to be gaped at by everyone in the house, Madame Zazou?" she asked imperiously. "I will not permit such liberties. When I am countess—"

"But you are not a countess yet, *ma chère,*" Madame said in a strangely calm voice. "And you would not wish to have your brains dashed out by a drapery rod. So, we continue. I have brought your things and we shall resume the fitting in here.

Isabelle and Jane, bring the screen from the other room."

Isabelle hastened to obey but stepped in her hurry on the trailing fabric of the dressing gown, pulling it off Phoebe's shoulders. Phoebe clutched the billowing folds and shrieked with fury.

"Madame Zazou! Do you hire only halfwits? Leave at once!" She pointed dramatically at Isabelle.

*"Mon Dieu!"* Madame pretended to look shocked and waggled a scolding finger at Isabelle as she steered her through the door, slamming it behind her with a resounding bang. She gave her assistant a conspiratorial smile.

"Go to Mr. Cully's shop and buy the silk she wants," she whispered. "Take the carriage and Robert for the parcels. And take Fig from Maman's chamber—he loves to ride. I will try to stick as many pins as possible into Phoebe."

"Very good, Madame! I will do my best."

Isabelle ran down the stairs—and then she remembered the red-haired man on the rope. Was he still there? And why had Madame said nothing at all about him?

She collected Robert, forgetting Fig, and headed out to the street, wondering where Gabriel, the houseman who was usually posted at the doors, might be—and then she heard a thump and a groan.

Running in the direction of the noise, she turned the back corner of the town house and saw Gabriel and the red-haired man, now on the ground, squaring off.

Robert, eager to watch the fisticuffs, bumped into Isabelle from behind.

"Beggin' your pardon, miss!"

"Oh, Robert, this is no time for pretty manners! Whatever shall we do?"

The two men circled, oblivious to everything but each other, their fists up and at the ready.

"We could douse 'em with water, miss. I have seen it done to fightin' dogs. Put a stop to it right quick," he said rather reluctantly.

"Well, then run to the stable and ask the coachman for . . . oh, never mind."

One lightning-fast punch from grizzled Gabriel had flattened the red-haired man.

The houseman spit on his bloodied knuckles. "Sorry you witnessed such dreadful violence, Miss Isabelle. But Madame told me to give 'im what for and I have done."

The man lying on the ground moaned and clutched his bleeding nose.

"Naow, naow," Gabriel said almost tenderly. "None of yer noise or I'll do it again. Up on yer feet. Tell us who ye be and who sent ye here."

The man looked at Isabelle, then at Gabriel, and stood up slowly. He staggered—somewhat theatrically, Isabelle thought—but it was enough to fool the older man for the second the intruder needed to shove between them and escape.

"Come back 'ere!" Gabriel shouted, about to run after him until Isabelle put a gentle hand on his arm.

"You must not leave your post, Gabriel. What if his confederate attempts the same trick?"

As if in answer, the rope that had been dangling from the roof of the neighboring house slipped to the ground. Whoever had been holding it had run away as well.

"Nasty lot," Gabriel growled. "Behavin' like barbarians, botherin' hinnocent young ladies. Wot is the world coming to?"

"If only I knew—"

"Well, Madame came down very quick before ye got here and said she would hexplain later. Let me just wash this blood from me hands and get ye on yer way—" He escorted Isabelle to the front of the house and sent Robert to have the carriage brought round from the mews on the other side of Clarges Street.

When the boy returned, he dispatched him to the neighboring house to warn the servants there of the intruders on the rooftop, should there be any remaining.

Isabelle went inside to fetch her bonnet, remembering Fig at last, whom she collected from Jehane while the carriage was made ready. She handed the little dog to Robert when he came back and put the bonnet somewhat carelessly upon her head, letting its blue ribbons trail over her shoulders.

The late afternoon sun felt wondrously warm upon her upturned face. A few minutes in it would do no harm, no matter what Madame had told her about preserving her complexion for all eternity.

She heard the agreeable rattle of the carriage wheels before she saw it. It was a barouche, a recent gift from another Venerable Admirer who had been most pleased with Madame's company. The dappled grays pulled up, looking very smart in their new harness.

The coachman gave her a shockingly familiar grin and a most improper wink. Not that Isabelle minded a bit, because Alf was Gabriel's twin, and she was equally fond of both.

The middle-aged brothers were identical in every particular, including their imposing height and neatly trimmed whiskers, except that Gabriel, a former pugilist, had had his nose broken twice and Alf never.

He assisted Isabelle into the carriage and let Robert swing himself up on the box beside him, clutching the wriggling Fig under one arm.

"A fine day, miss. Sorry about the disturbance. Them peepin' toms deserve to be thrashed. They have come round afore, but never one so bold as to swing on a rope."

"Yes, Alf. I do hope he does not return."

" 'Ave no fear, miss," he said cheerfully, slapping the horses on the rump with the reins. "Me and Gabe will murder 'im wif our bare hands. Just say the word."

Young Robert looked thrilled but Isabelle shuddered. "I fear for your immortal soul, Alf."

"Oh, right. Thou shalt not kill and all that. Well, it were only a thought."

She smiled at his cheerful bloodthirstiness and took in the passing scene. The fine day was drawing to a close but the streets were still thronged with people, coming and going on errands of their own.

Alf clucked to the horses and turned the carriage left, which made Robert and Fig slide toward him. The boy hit his iron-hard side with a thump.

"Easy, lad. That's where I broke me ribs not a month ago."

Robert looked at him with wide eyes. "How?"

"Now there is a story, lad, and no mistake!" Alf lowered his voice dramatically. "It were a midnight drear when I encountered a gang o' homicidalous highwaymen upon a lonely heath. They put up a vicious fight, they did, but I prevailed in the end. Them velvet-clad ruffians was rolling in the dust, very angry that I ruined their fine clothes, to say nuffink of breaking their elegant noses."

Robert listened raptly. Isabelle knew Alf had only fallen off a horse inside the stable, but she held her tongue.

She looked about for a certain narrow street that went its crooked way from the main thoroughfare. There, drapers and mercers sold their wares at bargain prices if one did not mind a bit of haggling. Madame had taught Isabelle how by her own steely-eyed example and she was eager to try out her skill, even if it would benefit only the unpleasant Miss Sharpe.

At the moment, many of the shopkeepers stood or sat outside, leaving the endless demands of miladies and maids to their assistants, while they enjoyed the mild evening breeze.

A few recognized Madame Zazou's new barouche, and many knew the pretty young woman who looked about from it, waving to friends and acquaintances in a carefree way, clutching her untied bonnet now and then to keep it on her head.

She called to Alf to turn at the lane and stop in front of a row of half-timbered buildings more than a century old, which leaned on one another like the ancient survivors of the Great Fire that they were.

Alf pulled up the horses gently and let Robert hitch them to a stout railing of wrought iron.

"Now, me lad, give me that there dog and assist

our Miss Mousey like the lady she is. And keep out o' the gutter muck."

The golden-haired boy leapt down to the cobblestones and offered his hand to Isabelle with a gentlemanly flourish.

She took it as she stepped down, giving him a regal nod that made him grin. "Thank you, Master Robert. Well done indeed. Now that I am safely upon *terra firma,* let us proceed to Mr. Cully's shop and see if he has the silk in question."

She gathered up her skirts in one hand to skip over the gutter—and looked up into the eyes of Nigel Wollaston.

# CHAPTER 9

*An amorous nature is betrayed . . .*

"Good afternoon, Miss Mousey."

Her heart stopped beating for a perilous second. "How—how did you know my name?"

Alf was looking at Mr. Wollaston suspiciously from his vantage point atop the coachman's box and Robert edged nearer to Isabelle. Fig barked furiously until Alf clapped one huge hand around his muzzle, leaving the dog just enough room to breathe.

"Fig—shut yer gob. Pardon me langwidge, miss."

Isabelle nodded, too flustered to be offended by anything. If this gentleman had somehow found her out, anyone might. She had hoped to conceal her identity as long as possible, but she had never expected an encounter like this. She had become used to being regarded as a person of no consequence and thus invisible.

Oh, well. She was invisible no more. But surely a

Londoner would never have heard of the Mouseys, who preferred the country—and certainly not of her, the last of the line, according to Lady Griselda.

"Forgive my forwardness," Nigel began, feeling very awkward, "but as we both know Madame Zazou—in a manner of speaking—um." He paused after the *um* for several excruciatingly long seconds. "Ah—she told me to simply introduce myself. My name is Nigel Wollaston."

"Good afternoon, Mr. Wollaston." Why—and how—had he followed her?

"Allow me to explain. She also told me that I might find you here. I rode ahead." He indicated his horse, an imposing bay gelding he had hastily borrowed from the Hyde Park stables, tied a little distance away, stamping its hooves and snorting inquisitively at Madame's grays. They snorted back and the mare on the right whinnied flirtatiously.

"That is not an explanation." Should she say that she knew who he was, thanks to Miss Sharpe? What if he had not been sent by Madame and was trying to gain her confidence for some unknown reason?

Nigel spoke quickly. "If you will permit me to accompany you inside, Miss Mousey, I have information from Madame to aid you in your purchase." He stopped—she did not look like she believed a word he had said. "And a note from her to you." He pulled it from his pocket and offered it to her with a flourish.

Whether or not she believed him, he *had* talked to Madame Zazou, after his return from a nearby coffeehouse and a fortuitous encounter with a scullery maid—Sukey was her name—sent out to sweep the front stairs of the house.

Persuaded by no more than a wink and a six-pence, Sukey had told him all that had just happened. Her dramatic account of the scar-faced intruder swinging upon the rope had surprised and shocked him.

Were the betting men of White's to blame? He remembered vaguely that William Browne had a servant with red hair—but did the fellow have a scar? While Nigel was thinking, the grizzled brute of a houseman had come out and told him roughly to be off.

Then Madame had suddenly appeared and told Gabriel—who was apparently the twin of the coachman, unless Nigel was seeing double—that it was quite all right, Nigel was welcome in her house.

She had handed him a note for Isabelle and given him directions to Mr. Cully's establishment—and, wonder of wonders, offered an invitation to dinner that Nigel could not very well refuse.

The houseman had seemed every bit as confused as he was but tugged on a nonexistent fore-lock and muttered an apology. Madame had given them both a gracious smile and gone back indoors.

"Oh—very well." Isabelle looked up at Alf and nodded reassuringly. "Thank you, Alf. Please wait here." She opened the note, which was no more than a few words to introduce the tall man at her side. There were no instructions as to her planned purchase, but she supposed that would all be explained later, as Nigel had promised.

"Well, Mr. Wollaston"—how pleasant it was to simply say his name!—"shall we go inside?"

Nigel glanced at Alf, who was looking at him with unnerving fierceness. It was just possible that he could best the man in a fair fight if he had to, but only just.

He had to admire Madame—the woman protected her house well and these twin guardians would make formidable opponents, despite not being in the first flush of youth.

And the little dog was just as formidable in his small way. Fig—if that was his name—glared at him as fiercely as the coachman did.

Nonetheless, someone had breached the ramparts, according to the scullery maid, and Nigel was sure there would be more such attempts in the future. He would have to discuss the matter with Madame, once he had gained her trust. He put aside the thought for the moment and walked Miss Mousey to the shop door.

A boy scampered out to open it, seeming to assume—Nigel was pleased—that he and Miss Mousey were a couple.

"Come in, sir—and miss."

The bell above the shop door jingled merrily as the trio entered, blinking as their eyes adjusted to the near darkness within. Bolts of lustrous silks gleamed from the shelves that lined the walls, and other, less costly materials were heaped higgledy-piggledy upon tables.

Robert immediately asked to be allowed to play with Billy Cully, the boy who had opened the door. Isabelle said yes, and Robert dashed behind the counter.

Mr. Andrew Cully, the stout shopkeeper, ceased cutting a length of cloth to peer at them over spectacles that sat crookedly on his nose.

"Miss Mousey! Always a welcome sight—you are as lovely as ever, though it is time you had a new dress, my girl. Something in eggshell blue? Or petal pink perhaps?"

"Someday, Mr. Cully—but today I need a Spitalfields silk in a most unusual shade—for one of Madame's customers." She stopped, not wanting to repeat Phoebe's moonbeams-and-magic description.

If Mr. Cully knew that a customer wanted something very much, the price was higher. He too had been taught to haggle, but by his French wife. He himself was English to the bone—bones that were well-padded with the beefsteaks and ale he bragged of consuming in great quantities. But he had married into a Huguenot family of silk weavers.

Mr. Cully nodded. "We have silk in every color, my dear." He waved a meaty hand at the shelves and tables to indicate that she might browse to her heart's content and turned to Nigel. "Something for the gentleman, then? May I show you a length of the rare Ovine Merino? Just the thing for a hunt coat—do you hunt, sir?"

"I do not." Nigel looked to Miss Mousey for guidance but she was absorbed in examining the goods upon the shelves.

"Ah. I see. You prefer indoor pastimes. It is always one or the other with gentlemen. Then do consider this brocade, sir—"

Damn it all. Mr. Cully had inadvertently spoken the truth, but the shopkeeper did not know it. Yet Nigel's face turned as scarlet as the gaudy length of figured silk the draper was running through his plump fingers.

"Indoor pastimes?" Isabelle inquired sweetly. "Why, Mr. Wollaston, what would those be?"

Had she actually asked such a leading question?

He could not quite believe her impudence. How could a staymaker's assistant address him as an equal? It was not done.

But she had just done it. It occurred to him that she was waiting for a reply. "Ahem—chess. And reading. I subscribe to a library, of course, when I am in town. . . ." He trailed off, feeling somewhat foolish. Surely some indelicate rumor concerning his private affairs had not reached Isabelle's innocent ears. He wanted to keep it that way. And he had not lied. He did enjoy chess and reading.

"And what was the last book you read, Mr. Wollaston?"

She was damnably curious. It was as if she wanted to know more about him, before he had had a chance to find out more about her. "Let me think—*The Decline and Fall of The Roman Empire*." There. That ought to give her the impression that he was a serious sort of fellow.

"Oh—Mr. Gibbon's book."

He raised an eyebrow. "Have you read it, Miss Mousey?"

She quoted a few lines that he seemed to remember, and he gaped at her, utterly astonished. "Yes, I have read it. But I thought it was overlong and rather wooden, even for a historical tome."

"Aha. Oho." He scarcely knew what to say next.

"You seem surprised, Mr. Wollaston," she said gravely. She had moved on to a different shelf and began to investigate the selection of materials upon it.

Mr. Cully padded after her in his shop slippers, still holding the scarlet silk and bent upon selling it to Nigel, who wished he would go away.

"It is not the sort of book that females generally read, Miss Mousey."

"Sir, if I may be so bold—" the shopkeeper said insinuatingly, proffering the silk once more. "Just feel the quality, if you would. Highly suitable for evening wear. Such a scarlet would be remarked upon at the most brilliant assembly."

"Indeed," Nigel said politely.

"Imagine leading the quadrille in this, sir." He held it up to Nigel's middle. "Oh, you would stand out indeed."

The thought made Nigel wince. "Thank you, Mr. Cully—but no. I am only here to assist the young lady. If you will excuse us—"

The stout draper sighed almost inaudibly. Obviously he had hoped to sell something to Nigel, taking him for a fop or a fool—Nigel was not sure which was more insulting.

"Oh, quite. I do understand, sir." Mr. Cully began to move away. "Perhaps some other time. Just say the word and I will send Billy round with whatever you might require in the way of goods."

Nigel turned back to Isabelle, who was running a hand over a length of golden velvet, as if stroking the fur of a much-loved animal. Ah, if only he could be that fortunate Beast and she, his Beauty—he drew in a sharp breath and told himself not to entertain such thoughts.

Miss Mousey's trust would be won only by scrupulous observance of every propriety. There could be no longing gazes, no accidental brushes of his hand against her sweetly curved form—nothing whatsoever of that sort.

He rested his hand upon a scratchy bolt of wool

as if to chastise it for wanting to caress her, as she had caressed the velvet.

But—oh, hellish temptation—*her* hand brushed his as she looked at the hound's-tooth wool.

"It would make a fine jacket for Robert," she said softly. "He will outgrow the one he has by autumn." She looked up, wide-eyed, for the briefest of seconds after she spoke.

Her touch was enough to make his knees go weak. And it was the second time she had touched him. He tried to think nothing of it—damn it all, he was experienced in such matters.

She was not. She was young. Innocent. Or so she appeared.

*Was* Miss Isabelle Mousey so very innocent? The ardent glow in her eyes betrayed an amorous nature, gently bred though she was. And he still had no idea how or why she had come to live in Madame's unusual household.

Nigel's mind was racing and so was his heart. He could not recollect any female of his acquaintance causing him to feel such tenderness.

Could this be love? He rather liked it so far. Certainly he would have to find out more about her, for she was not to be trifled with and he did not want to face the wrath of a beetle-browed papa discovering that he, Nigel, had compromised his darling daughter.

She must have run away to London from somewhere, and someone must wonder where she was. Perhaps she would inadvertently drop some clue at dinner tonight. He could ask his solicitor, Mr. Boggles, to commence an investigation, but Boggles would need more than just her name—

His thoughts were interrupted by a soft "Oh!"

Miss Mousey seemed to have found what she was looking for, an odd sort of double-colored silk that was under several other much larger bolts, and tugged at it.

"Allow me," said Nigel, pulling it—and everything else on the shelf—into a tangled heap on the floor. Mr. Cully came running.

"Sir, you do not know your own strength."

Nigel felt like a fool. Now he would have to buy the scarlet silk, just to make amends. The draper called for his boy, who appeared from behind the counter with Robert and set to picking up and folding straightaway.

"Oh dear—I do apologize, Mr. Cully." Isabelle gave him a dimpled smile.

"No need, no need," the draper replied. "Is that the shot silk you were wanting? A very fine fabric, Miss Mousey. Very fine indeed."

He held it up to the waning light of day from the front window, showing off its silvery sheen with an expert flourish. Nigel wondered who would wear the dress it was destined to become.

Isabelle nodded and began to bargain, giving Nigel a slightly abashed look as she did so. Clearly she was not bred to such vulgar discourse, but there was an unmistakable gleam in her eye. He had no doubt she would get the better of Mr. Cully.

But the stout draper held his ground, positively rhapsodic on the subject of this particular silk. "It is like gossamer, miss. From a fairy loom, woven by moonlight—"

"And how much is it, Mr. Cully?" Isabelle asked.

He mentioned a price. Nigel wanted to laugh. The fairies were clearing an extraordinary profit. He would look into investing in gossamer and buying shares of moonlight at the earliest possible opportunity.

Isabelle raised an elegant eyebrow. "Mr. Cully, that is much too dear. I will give you—" She named a much lower figure.

The draper looked shocked. "Oh, Miss Mousey—but I cannot go so low. I will be ruined at this rate!" He cast a glance at the tall man at her side.

Nigel was looking about nonchalantly, keeping well away from other potential avalanches, the draper noted with approval. Not all gentlemen would have been so courteous, and he hoped to keep the custom of this one, if only because Miss Mousey seemed to like the fellow.

He sighed theatrically. "Well, well. For you. But do not tell Madame Zazou. If I end my days in the poorhouse, she will be to blame. That is a Frenchwoman for you. I suppose she has taught you everything."

"No, not everything—" Isabelle looked up to see Mr. Wollaston eyeing her speculatively and blushed. Did he think that Madame was something other than a corsetière? Well, he could go to the devil if he did, no matter how handsome he was.

She rummaged in her reticule for the money Madame had given her as Mr. Cully cut the goods to the requested length.

"Ah—I will take the scarlet silk after all," Nigel said quickly.

"Very good, sir."

His boy made up two parcels of thin, crackling paper and folded the fine fabric carefully within each, whipping string over and around to make handles while his father looked on proudly.

"Thank you, Billy. Come along, Robert." The

golden-haired lad picked up her parcel and carried it with comical pomp, looking for all the world like a page at a royal court, happy to serve the princess he idolized.

Miss Mousey seemed to have that effect upon every male she encountered, Nigel thought.

# CHAPTER 10

*The wonders of love . . .*

Alf was waiting for them—and he had been kept waiting too long, by the disgruntled expression upon his face. Nigel searched his pockets and came up with a few shillings.

Though a scowl like that deserved no reward, Nigel gave him the coins anyway, in keeping with his plan to ingratiate himself with every member of Madame Zazou's household.

Alf seemed surprised, even pleased. "Thank you, m'lud."

Nigel nodded affably. "You have been patient. No doubt your supper is getting cold and I suppose the missus is waiting."

Alf's expression changed to one of wistfulness. "There is no missus, sir. I sup at the inn and I sleep in Madame's stable."

"I see." Nigel thought of Dolly, the coffee house wench and her ready laugh, and smiled. Perhaps he could contrive to introduce her to Alf by the morrow and get the man on his side. He would need to have eyes and ears everywhere to inform him of suspicious occurrences and keep his betting friends at bay.

Would they try their luck with Miss Mousey as well? The thought had not occurred to him until now, and he found it troubling. He vowed to stay as close as he could to her—but how was he to do that without arousing Madame Zazou's suspicions?

A flower seller sidled up to him. "Flowers for the lydy, sir? Fresh spring vi'lets? Very pretty they are—as pretty as herself."

Nigel nodded and took a posy from the woman's outstretched hand, giving it to Miss Mousey as he dug in his pocket for a coin—and came up empty-handed. Alf grinned and tossed him one of the shillings he had received, which Nigel presented to the flower seller.

"Keep the change. And thank you, Alf. I shall repay you."

"No need, sir."

Isabelle beamed with pleasure, sniffing the fragrant violets. "Good-bye, Mr. Wollaston."

"Good-bye, Miss Mousey. I must return to my apartments but I look forward with great pleasure to dining with you and Madame Zazou." He watched with delight as her lips parted slightly with surprise. "Did Madame not mention it in her note? She invited me to come at eight tonight."

She dimpled in a delectable way—ah, if he could only kiss the pretty little curves that framed her smile. Once would not be enough.

"No, she did not. But you will not regret accepting her invitation. Madame cooks a fine *coq au vin* every Thursday. And her cellar is much praised by gentlemen—" She broke off, obviously not wishing to give him the wrong impression.

Alf looked over his brawny shoulder and gave Nigel a knowing wink. The coachman made the harnesses jingle a bit to cover Isabelle's embarrassment. "Well, sir—Miss Mousey—we must be off. Madame Zazou will be hexpecting us."

"Of course." Nigel helped Isabelle in, keeping his parcel tucked under his arm.

Robert scrambled up to the box and the coachman gave the horses' rumps a good slap with the reins. Their hooves clip-clopped smartly, setting a brisk pace over the cobblestones as the carriage turned the corner.

Nigel watched them go, hoping Miss Mousey would favor him with another of those dazzling smiles. But he was not so lucky this time.

He walked to his borrowed horse, untied it, and swung into the saddle, considering his next move as he rode through the streets.

There was the dinner to come. He would inform Madame of the bet, of course, though it was very likely she already knew of it. Like Jeremy, she was in a profession where gossip was rife.

In return for her silence on the subject of Phoebe, he would offer her and her household his protection—this might mean hiring a few Bow Street runners to help guard the house on Clarges Street, but the expense would be worth it and would benefit her and her business. Nigel was certain she would agree.

He wondered idly if Miss Sharpe did wear an Invisible Arrangement. Though Phoebe's person was otherwise slight, it was entirely possible that her remarkable bosom was her own. Women came in many wonderful shapes, as his amorous adventures had proved.

However, he had a feeling that Miss Mousey possessed by far the finest figure in London, though her modest dress only hinted at it. Another thought occurred to him: did Isabelle wear an Invisible Arrangement? He dismissed the question immediately as unworthy, to say nothing of unimportant, and rode on.

Meanwhile, at the house on Clarges Street, the fitting session proceeded apace. Madame Zazou had soothed Phoebe's fretfulness with more wine, which loosened her tongue to the point of indiscretion.

The girl went on and on about Bertie—his fortune, his houses, his stable, his habits—and her chances of marrying him.

"And—oh, Madame—there is a bet—about my bosom—and whether I wear an Invisible Arrangement. I know you will not tell a soul, but what if Bertie finds out?"

"Finds out what, Miss Sharpe?" Madame asked nonchalantly, as if she had not already heard about the bet. In any case, the earl could be no stranger to feminine artifice and womanly wiles at his age.

"He says I must always tell him the truth, Madame," Phoebe blurted out. "He says that real lovers have no s-secrets and that he will love me forever if I am pure and true and all that rot—" She broke off, making a noise somewhere between a sob and a grunt.

Madame was nonplussed. What could she possibly say to that? The English were really very strange.

"I am pure, Madame—and I am a virgin, no matter what gossip you may have heard."

"I have heard nothing on that subject," Madame replied carefully.

"And I am true to the earl, in my fashion. But to have no secrets from him—how can he ask that of me? No woman of sense is honest about every little thing, not when men are allowed to behave as if they owned us all."

"You have a point, Miss Sharpe." For once, Phoebe had said something intelligent. The girl was ill-tempered and gave herself dreadful airs, but her plight was the same as any other woman's: men ruled the world and the rules were made by men.

Phoebe wiped away a tear with the back of her hand, not bothering with her handkerchief—though she would need that to blow her nose, Madame thought, practical as always.

"And now I must worry about this ridiculous bet—no matter who wins or what happens, I shall be called a liar. And Bertie will no longer love me!"

"Do you love him?"

Phoebe nodded. "Of course—not. I just want to be a countess more than anything!"

"*Bien.* That is the way of the world. I cannot argue. But if you do not love the earl, why do you care whether he loves you?"

Isabelle entered the room as if she were waltzing on air, still carrying the posy of violets Nigel had given her. "Ah, love! Love is wonderful, is it not?"

# CHAPTER 11

*A female within pouncing distance . . .*

"As it happens, we were discussing that very subject," Phoebe said peevishly. "Are you in love, Miss Mousey? Has some strapping Billingsgate fishmonger pledged his trout to you?"

"I beg your pardon?"

"I meant his troth!" Phoebe shot her a sulky look. By way of explanation, Madame nodded ever so slightly at the decanter of cordial that the girl had nearly emptied.

"No—no one has pledged anything." Isabelle hastily set Nigel's posy aside, hoping the violets would not wilt before Phoebe departed. He was sweet to have given her flowers, but she supposed he did such things all the time. A mere staymaker's assistant, as he thought her to be, would not hold his attention for long. "Why would they, Miss Sharpe?"

"Men remark upon your beauty when you are out

on the streets. I have overheard more than one—"
She broke off, not wanting to admit that she walked
on the same streets, shopped at the same stores, as
the other girl. But she had spoken the truth—men
did notice Miss Mousey.

Still, a proper lady would not reveal an emotion
as base as jealousy the way she had just done, Phoebe
thought bitterly, resentful of her station in life as a
mere squire's daughter.

However, Miss Mousey's station in life was much
humbler. But that cheering thought only reminded
Phoebe that she had not yet improved her own—
her hoped-for marriage to the earl was in jeopardy
and all because of that stupid, stupid bet.

"I—I was not aware that they did, Miss Sharpe."
Isabelle shrank from Madame's sharp gaze. Why
was she studying Isabelle so intently? She had sent
Mr. Wollaston to find her, after all, and even invited
him to dinner tonight. Surely she had done nothing untoward.

Phoebe only shrugged. She stepped into the muslin mock-up of the dress Madame and the modiste
had designed, pulling it up carelessly and loosen-
ing a few pins, which Isabelle discreetly picked up.

"Is this the last of the ten I ordered, Madame?"

"It is." The Frenchwoman took the pins from Isa-
belle's hand and adjusted the puff of one sleeve.
"Do you know, Isabelle, you never did answer Miss
Sharpe's question. Are you in love?"

Isabelle gave a guilty start. She felt—different,
certainly, in a giddy way, but that was not necessar-
ily love. She knew nothing at all about Mr. Wollaston,
however charming, courteous, witty, well-spoken,
handsome, and somewhat annoyingly sure of himself he seemed to be. No. She was not in love.

Take a Trip Back to the
Romantic Regency Era
of the Early 1800's

**4 FREE
BOOKS
ARE
YOURS!**

# 4 *FREE*
## *Zebra Regency Romances!*
(A $19.96 VALUE!)

**Plus You'll Save Every Month With
Convenient Home Delivery!**

# We'd Like to Invite You to Subscribe to Zebra's Regency Romance Book Club and Send You 4 Free Books as Your Introduction! (Worth $19.96!)

If you're a Regency lover, imagine the joy of getting 4 FREE Zebra Regency Romances and then the chance to have these lovely stories delivered to your home each month at the lowest price available! Well, that's our offer to you and here's how you benefit by becoming a Regency Romance subscriber:

- *4 FREE Introductory Regency Romances are delivered to your doorstep (you only pay for shipping & handling)*
- *4 BRAND NEW Regencies are then delivered each month (usually before they're available in bookstores)*
- *Subscribers save almost $4.00 off the cover price every month*
- *You also receive a FREE monthly newsletter, which features author profiles, discounts, subscriber benefits, book previews and more*
- *There's no risks or obligations…in other words, you can cancel whenever you wish with no questions asked*

Join the thousands of readers who enjoy the savings and convenience offered to Regency Romance subscribers. After your initial introductory shipment, you'll receive 4 brand-new Zebra Regency Romances each month to examine for 10 days. Then, if you decide to keep the books, you pay the preferred subscriber's price, plus shipping and handling.

## It's a no-lose proposition, so return the FREE BOOK CERTIFICATE today!

A $19.96 value – **FREE** No obligation to buy anything – ever.
**4 FREE BOOKS** are waiting for you! Just mail in the certificate below!

# FREE BOOK CERTIFICATE

***YES!*** Please rush me 4 FREE Zebra Regency Romances (I only pay $1.99 for shipping and handling).I understand that each month thereafter I will be able to preview 4 brand-new Regency Romances FREE for 10 days. Then, if I should decide to keep them, I will pay the money-saving preferred subscriber's price for all 4… (that's a savings of 20% off the retail price), plus shipping and handling. I may return any shipment within 10 days and owe nothing, and I may cancel this subscription at any time.

Name _____

Address _____ Apt._____

City _____ State _____ Zip _____

Telephone (____) _____

Signature _____

(If under 18, parent or guardian must sign)

Offer limited to one per household and not to current subscribers. Terms, offer and prices subject to change. Orders subject to acceptance by Regency Romance Book Club. Offer Valid in the U.S. only.　　RN104A

REGENCY ROMANCE BOOK CLUB
Zebra Home Subscription Service, Inc.
P.O. Box 5214
Clifton NJ 07015-5214

PLACE
STAMP
HERE

"Certainly not. But I had been thinking about that fascinating emotion when I entered. In a theoretical sense, of course. Whatever would poets do without love to write about?"

Madame Zazou sniffed. "They might have to work for a living, like ordinary mortals. And speaking of that, you must help me complete Miss Sharpe's dress."

Isabelle nodded and stood ready as Madame resumed pinning the small sleeve. Phoebe raised her slender arms above her head to check the fit, looking very pretty indeed.

Was it fair that such a female was within pouncing distance of Nigel? It did not seem fair to Isabelle, not in the least. She had a feeling that Phoebe might set her cap at *him* should anything happen to the old earl.

But then she remembered Nigel's adoring gaze upon her and felt better. She looked over Phoebe's shoulder at Madame, who gave her an odd smile.

At that moment, Isabelle remembered the intruder who had so suddenly interrupted the first fitting. Had anything else happened while she was gone? She could not very well ask Madame in Phoebe's presence and the question would have to wait.

# CHAPTER 12

*Castles in the air . . .*

An hour or so later, Nigel had returned to the apartments he presently occupied at Albany Court. He would look into renting here on a permanent basis at the earliest possible opportunity. Nigel liked being conveniently close to dear old Bertie—and now, to Isabelle.

His valet had laid out evening clothes of a sober color and cut for a dinner he had decided not to attend the moment Madame Zazou had invited him to her house.

He would not miss such company—investors and speculators with ingenious new ideas for spending his uncle's surplus cash instead of their own. Nigel had sent Conway forth with a note extending his sincere regrets.

He looked over the clothes. "Very good, Conway," he murmured to himself. "Dashing but not disreputable. Exactly the impression I hope to make."

The man had brought up hot water for the bath that awaited him. Nigel stripped and tested it with a toe. Ah. It was precisely at what he called thinking temperature—and he planned to loll in it for a good while and do just that.

He stepped in and sat down, allowing his long legs to dangle outside, resting them on a rolled towel set upon the edge for that purpose. He squeezed out a washcloth floating in the water and scrubbed his face and neck with vigor.

Conway had shaved him well and closely before leaving to deliver the note, and then doused him with a strong scent before Nigel could protest that it was fit only for a pimp. He had coughed, though, and his eyes had watered mightily. Conway seemed pleased.

"It is powerful stuff, m'lud," the valet said proudly. "Distilled from rare herbs and flowers by me own mother. Only tuppence a bottle."

Nigel had heard much of the enterprising Mother Conway, who did a brisk business in other potent spirits that caused headaches in the morning, as well as potions that cured them. The vile fragrance that his valet had splashed on him was something new.

Fortunately, hot water washed it away. Nigel slid lower in the tub, wondering what Miss Mousey was doing at that moment. He recalled the moment he had seen her last, not turning her head as the carriage clattered away from Mr. Cully's shop on its way to Madame's house, as he hoped she would bestow another charming smile.

He thought about how charming she would look in *his* carriage, though he did not keep a carriage in London yet. He imagined her upon the steps of *his* house, though he did not have a house, returning from a pleasant afternoon of shopping.

He envisioned her within the parlor of this imaginary dwelling, perhaps at the pianoforte, playing a romantic melody while they whiled away the hours in sparkling conversation—how pleasant it would be.

Miss Mousey had the breeding to be his wife, of that he had no doubt. Her manners, her mien, gave away her gentle upbringing—here he gave a heartfelt sigh. Her milieu raised many questions.

How had she come to Madame Zazou's and why did she remain there? Did she have parents and did they approve of where she lived? Had she been cast out for some youthful indiscretion?

No doubt she had learned much that was unsavory about the so-called polite world in such a place, and he had no doubt that Isabelle knew the intimate details of every scandal of the season. Yet her essential innocence had somehow been preserved, a quality that was rare indeed in the circles in which he moved.

He reflected for the second time that day upon how powerfully it attracted him. As did her other qualities: Intelligence. Charm. A quiet wit that was all her own and nothing like the cynical jests of the fashionable belles and philandering wives of the *ton*.

His friends would envy him so rare a prize. He could tell that from the fellows who adored her now. Though Alf and his brother Gabriel and even Mr. Cully were certainly not gentlemen, they were goodhearted fellows and true sons of England. It was

obvious that they worshipped her—and he planned
to do no less—perhaps because she seemed to have
a gift for seeing the best in everyone.

He wondered if she saw anything in him—and if
so, what? Nigel sighed and adjusted his position.

The sparkle in her eyes spoke of a taste for adventure uncommon in a female of gentle upbringing. Living amid the hustle and bustle of London,
as she was now by some happenstance he had yet
to discover, did not seem to faze her in the slightest.

Polite society might be taken aback by her bold-
ness—but he could well imagine her making conversation with the Prince Regent himself. Not that
he wanted her to meet that dissolute individual,
whom he did not know personally in any case.

He sloshed about in the bath, thinking it over.
First things first: Nigel would be happy to pay Mr.
Boggles and his ink-stained clerks to pore over
church records and dusty peerages and find out
what they could about Miss Mousey. Jeremy could
undoubtedly ferret out more information from his
many sources, and perhaps the man's dear Grace,
tireless gossip that she was, knew something.

The silly business of the wager at White's would
be swiftly resolved, he knew, and he could concentrate on Isabelle from then on.

His rambling thoughts moved to a bedroom
that did not exist, in the house he did not have,
luxuriously appointed for the ease and enjoyment
of a man and his mistress.

Only he wanted Isabelle to be his wife. The
thought shocked him by its suddenness.

Yes, he had had enough of mistresses and *af-*

*faires de coeur* and the tempestuous nonsense that invariably accompanied them.

Upon coming to London several seasons ago, Nigel had done what society expected of a young man not ready to marry, pursued this beauty and that, even kept an actress for a few stormy months, but not one had ever made him feel the way he did now. He was happy in Isabelle's presence—simply and perfectly happy.

She had captured his heart in an instant—well, in an hour—by being her own charming self.

To have her as a devoted, intelligent, pretty wife to love above all others was what he truly wanted, someone to adore and cherish, someone to come home to and sleep with each night . . . oh, yes.

Nigel knew without a doubt that he was in love. There was no other name for this wonderful feeling. He did not know how it had happened or why it had happened so fast but it *had* happened—for the first time in his life. All that remained was to convince her of it.

His mind returned to the bedroom he had planned. He mentally added a fireplace framed in fine marble, ablaze with an imaginary fire, as he was shivering at the moment.

A colossal bed was turned down and warmed for them, heaped with swansdown pillows and linens trimmed in exquisite lace—women liked such fripperies, though he only cared that the bed was long enough.

The canopy would be bedecked with pink damask draperies, and perhaps—yes, a few cupids could be carved upon the headboard for romantic effect. But not the revoltingly coy sort and not the sort that leered—he would have to give the wood-carver careful instructions about the cupids.

By the time the water was completely cold, Nigel had built a splendid castle in the air for Miss Mousey and himself and provided it with every comfort, including a staff of twelve just to keep up with the dusting.

He assumed she would marry him—and why would she not? Gently bred though Isabelle was, she was undoubtedly poor, though that was no fault of hers. Nigel had thirty thousand pounds in the five percents, which he would be happy to lavish upon her.

He clambered out, still shivering as he reached for a towel and dried himself, grinning. There would be children, of course, given the blissful nights to come in the imaginary bedroom, but he would leave the nursery decoration up to her.

It was a delightful fantasy—and Nigel intended to make it come true.

The object of his amorous daydreams was herself splashing about in a bath in a back bedroom and had lugged the hot water for it upstairs without assistance. As Madame had headed straight for the kitchen after Phoebe's departure to supervise the dinner preparations, Isabelle had not learned whether the intruder of the morning had returned and had decided not to worry about it.

She settled lower into the delicious warmth of her bath, enjoying the fragrance of the violets Nigel had given her, which she had placed in a nearby vase.

Isabelle began to sing an old song, happy to be

alone. "If I were queen, oh, if I were queen. . . ."
She felt rather giddy still and took a deep breath
to calm herself—the sweet scent of the violets tickled her nose most pleasantly.

She was looking forward to dinner.

# CHAPTER 13

*An attempt upon her virtue . . .*

Was Madame determined to impress Mr. Wollaston? And why? Isabelle had not spoken to her employer long enough to ask why he had been invited to dinner in the first place.

She looked into the dining room, where a snow-white tablecloth of damask covered the long table, set with delicate china and ornate silver. These precious forks and spoons and knives had been retrieved by Madame from a hidey-hole under her bed that no one knew about. They had been hastily polished by Robert, who was thrilled to be entrusted with this solemn responsibility, under the watchful eye of the cook.

Madame had even lent Isabelle a new dress of pink silk and pearl earrings. She now inspected her protégée with a critical but friendly eye, tugging her sash a little more tightly and smoothing

Isabelle's honey-gold hair. *"Tu est très jolie.* The pearls are not a perfect match, but there is a whole face in between, *n'est-ce pas?"*

Isabelle blushed. Madame was not one to give compliments lightly, and for her to say that Isabelle looked very pretty was high praise.

"All is in readiness. Robert and the cook shall wait upon us. I have given the housemaids the evening off."

Madame was in a jolly sort of mood, Isabelle thought. The dinner would be more intimate without so many servants coming and going, and that was all to the good.

Promptly at eight there came a knock on the door, and Gabriel answered it. Isabelle heard him greet Mr. Wollaston and relieve him of gloves and hat before Nigel came to the dining room, where she and Madame were waiting.

He entered, and her heart leapt. But Isabelle merely nodded as Madame greeted him in voluble French, wondering if he understood it all. She looked at the table, making sure that everything was just so, feeling unaccountably shy. Chatting with him in Mr. Cully's shop was much easier than making small talk in Madame's presence, she reflected.

And the room seemed a trifle too warm. It would not do for him to see her blush or behave missishly in any way. "Madame, might I open the French doors to the balcony? The evening is very fine."

*"Certainement."* Madame looked at Nigel. "If our guest is agreeable."

He nodded, seeming amused by all this formality. Isabelle went to the glass-paned doors that opened onto a small balcony, decorated with pots of flowering plants that gave off a subtle fragrance. She took a deep breath, composing herself, and went back in.

Robert appeared at the dining room door, dressed in livery that was just a little too big for him. Madame turned him this way and that, inspecting the sleeves and hem.

"*Zut!* Well, you will grow into it. Tell the cook we are ready."

He dashed out, shining his buttons with the cuffs. Isabelle tried not to smile.

After Nigel had poured the wine and offered gallant toasts to them both, Madame rose from the table to ring the kitchen. With the bellpull in hand, she gave it a single quick tug and waited. And waited.

"There is a system to it," Isabelle hastened to explain. "One rings once for the first course, twice for the second, and so on."

"I see. An eminently sensible arrangement," Nigel said approvingly.

"Hmph," said Madame. "Robert is much quicker."

The cook finally appeared, bearing a large majolica tureen in the shape of an impossibly plump hen. This she placed in front of Madame, who had returned to her place at the head of the table.

Madame lifted off the lid and sniffed appreciatively, waiting for the cook to leave before she spoke. "*Bien.* She has not ruined it. Mr. Wollaston, do you like *coq au vin?*"

"I have never had the dish, but I have heard of it, Madame. It smells very good."

She served it up and there was no sound but the clink of silver and appreciative murmurs for several moments. Several more courses were rung for according to the signaling system and appeared; and were duly consumed between such talk as they could manage. Isabelle and Nigel exchanged looks from time to time, and smiles, and the salt.

It was all very awkward, Isabelle thought, but she was delighted to see him again so soon. To dine by candlelight with him, even in Madame's presence, was romantic in the extreme. She took small bites and ate little, not wanting to appear hoydenish or greedy, but Nigel ate with gusto.

"You have a hearty appetite, Mr. Wollaston," said Madame, obviously pleased that he was enjoying himself. "Has it been satisfied?"

"Indeed it has, Madame. In every way." Well, not quite. If he could but sit alone with Isabelle, Nigel thought, and stroke her soft cheek, and whisper sweet nothings into her dear ear, then he would be satisfied in every way. He looked into her eyes, wishing he could tell her as much.

Madame rang the bellpull several times and waited a moment. When there was no reply, she rose and left the room, calling for Robert.

"Brace yourself," Isabelle whispered conspiratorially. "There is blancmange."

Madame returned, followed by Robert, proudly bearing a quivering white shape decorated with berries and syrup. The silver tray he carried it upon was heavy and he struggled to keep the dessert level.

"Oh, do be careful, Robert—"

"I shall, miss—oh!" The tray tipped too much for the boy to right it again. Nigel reached out to help him but the blancmange slithered off its platter as if it were alive. In another second, it went over the edge and landed on the floor with a squelching sound. An awful silence fell.

"Oh dear—I am dreadfully sorry, Madame. It was not the boy's fault. Do forgive me—"

She waved away Nigel's concern. "It is nothing. We will have gateaux and coffee in the drawing room. Robert—"

The boy kneeled, attempting to grasp the white blobs with no success.

Isabelle giggled. "Robert, stop that. You cannot pick up a blancmange with your hands."

*"Non!"* said Madame a little impatiently. "Go find Fig. He will enjoy this unexpected treat and the carpet will be like new when he is finished licking it."

"But it will trouble his digestion, Madame," the boy said anxiously.

She shrugged and rose from her chair. "That dog has eaten much worse." She swept out, leaving the mess on the floor, and the boy followed. "I will join you in the drawing room shortly," she said over her shoulder.

Isabelle knew by the sound of their footsteps that Madame had gone down the back way to the kitchen, with Robert on her heels. They were alone at last—had Madame arranged it of a purpose?

Nigel broke the awkward silence. "Well, then . . . shall we?"

"Shall we what, Mr. Wollaston?"

"Proceed to the drawing room." Nigel offered Isabelle his arm. She took it and led him there.

He looked about as they entered. The room had been decorated in the French taste, with fanciful wallpaper and porcelain figurines by the score. An ormolu clock ticked upon the mantel and suddenly let out a chime that made him jump. Isabelle seemed to be used to it.

"It does that every fifteen minutes."

"I see. Is there a way to stop it?"

She shook her head. A honey-gold lock came loose and Nigel had to force himself not to brush it back over her ear. Taking her arm was one thing, caressing her hair was quite another.

"Please do sit down." She indicated the largest of the gilded chairs, which was scarcely big enough for her.

Nigel, who had eaten rather too well, wished he could sprawl luxuriously as he did upon his uncle's furniture, but he resigned himself to remaining upright. He sat down carefully and stretched his long legs out.

Isabelle took a smaller chair, upholstered in a deep pink velvet that set off her gown very nicely. She smiled at him. "Are you quite comfortable, Mr. Wollaston?"

He nodded. "Quite. Thank you, Miss Mousey." He wondered how one broached the subject of eternal love in circumstances like these and decided to stick to something lighter for the moment.

"I very much enjoyed our time together this afternoon," he began.

She smiled again, showing those damnable dimples. "As did I."

"Yes."

He had never felt so tongue-tied or so silly. It occurred to him that this awkwardness was also part of being in love. When feelings were strong and sincere, reducing them to mere words became very difficult. Yet words were all that he had at the moment. He could not very well pull her onto his lap and kiss her senseless, which was what he wished to do. Madame might enter at any moment.

He stared at her dumbly, drinking in her loveliness, admiring her figure in the shimmering pale pink gown, and letting his gaze linger upon her shining eyes. Damn. What poetry could he quote, what eloquence could he summon to praise her radiance? He racked his brain.

"That gown—suits you." Damn, damn. That was hardly eloquent. Still, she seemed flattered.

"Thank you, Mr. Wollaston. Madame was kind enough to lend it to me from our stock."

Ah. She could not afford even this demure dress. He wanted to offer her all the money he had to buy every pretty thing her heart desired, satisfy her every need, please her, tease her. . . . Damn, damn, damn.

There were soft words spoken in French in the hall, and then a tremendous clatter. Isabelle giggled charmingly and whispered, "Madame is telling Robert to make noise and give us time. She must expect to find us in each other's arms."

"Ah—the boy speaks French," Nigel said, knowing that the remark was inane but unable to come up with a better one. Perhaps he should have been more forward and pulled her onto his lap after all. Were they to be found in a compromising position, he would have to marry her. Why had he not thought of that?

Robert coughed conspicuously as he crossed the threshold, bearing a tiered epergne filled with assorted tiny cakes, beautifully iced. In the interest of safety, Madame carried the tall silver coffeepot and set it down upon a small table that Nigel had not noticed, where fragile cups and saucers, small spoons and serviettes had been already set out.

"Voyla!" crowed Robert. "Lay cat toes!"

Madame gave him an amused look. "Not cat toes, Robert. *Gateaux*. Once more, if you please. *Voilà! Les gateaux!*"

"That is what I said, Madame."

She laughed in a kind way and ruffled his hair. "Well, Rome was not built in a day."

"What does that mean?" he asked.

"Nothing, really. Have a cake, *chéri.*"

The boy selected the biggest of the small treats and stuffed it into his mouth with evident delight before offering the epergne to Isabelle and Robert.

"Not like that, Robert," Isabelle said with amusement. "You must set it on the table and people will put the cakes they choose onto those little plates."

"Oh. Sorry, miss. And sir."

Nigel was highly amused when she took a little cake anyway and popped it into her mouth. He followed her lead, smiling at Robert as best he could with a mouthful of very tasty crumbs. The boy smiled back and took the epergne to the table, pleased to have done his duty.

Nigel watched Madame pour coffee and accepted a cup, which he very much needed.

She gave one to Isabelle and sat down with her own, clinking a tiny spoon in the dark liquid to mix up the extraordinary amount of sugar she had added.

"And now—the explanations."

Isabelle looked at her with surprise, having entirely forgotten the strange events of the morning during dinner. Odd, that—certainly it was not every day that one saw apelike men on ropes swinging by one's windows. She blamed her distracted state on Nigel's presence. How could she think with him giving her those adoring looks? Not that longing glances amounted to anything, she reminded herself firmly.

"The intruder . . ." Madame began.

Isabelle's mind wandered again. What explanation could there be? The man had not been caught—Gabriel would have told her if he had. . . . The ormolu clock ticked heavily in the ensuing silence.

The older woman continued to talk. Robert, who had remained in the room, listened with wide eyes. Within a few minutes, Isabelle knew everything that Madame knew of the bet concerning Phoebe and the need to protect the information that might simultaneously ruin her least favorite customer's prospects of marriage and Madame's business.

"It will not be long before the personal measurements of other young ladies become the subject of new bets, Mr. Wollaston."

Between his worries about his uncle and his interest in Miss Mousey, that had not occurred to him. He put on an expression of deep concern.

"Indeed it might, Madame Zazou. This must be nipped in the bud."

"Gabriel successfully repelled the first intruder, but others are sure to try their luck, perhaps as soon as tonight. The information that they seek must be shown at White's within a week, or the bet is off."

Nigel nodded. Madame knew more than he did. Like Jeremy, she heard virtually all of the *ton* gossip immediately—though, unlike Jeremy, she did not seem to delight in spreading it herself.

"Therefore, I propose that you stay here for a few days. You can pretend to be a friend of Alf's and help with the horses, or some such thing. The maids did not see you enter, as I gave most of them the evening off. But you would do well to ignore them later and say as little as possible."

Isabelle's eyes grew wider than Robert's. Madame had planned everything without saying a word to her—but why was the Frenchwoman telling Nigel of this? He must have some personal interest in the matter that would be revealed, probably within minutes. Oh, why had Isabelle been silly enough to think he was interested in *her*?

It would not be quite proper for him to stay in Madame's house—but then there was nothing quite proper about the way they lived. She supposed it would not matter if he remained incognito, like her.

"The next men who try may well be far more ingenious about gaining entry," Nigel said thoughtfully. "We must plan our defense. Mount the battlements, as it were."

The Frenchwoman looked at him approvingly. *"Exactement.* But only one small thing need be hidden—the notebook in which I keep my clients' most confidential information. First I lock its covers and then I lock it inside my desk." She pulled out the small keys on the chain around her neck to show to him.

"My dear Madame, locks of such diminutive size would be easy to break," Nigel said tactfully.

"Of course. It is getting inside the house that we must make difficult. Gabriel guards the front door—his chamber is only a few steps from it, behind the cloakroom. Alf can watch the garden from his quarters in the stables, and you shall guard the back door. The previous coachman used to sleep in a small bedroom near it, but no one has used that room for a long time."

Isabelle was surprised to hear of its existence—she had known nothing of it. "What will Mr. Wollaston do for clothes, Madame?"

"He can wear the coachman's old coat and hat. And if his own become somewhat dirty, it will go unremarked."

Madame continued. "You can come and go from there without anyone really noticing, Mr. Wollaston. It will be quite convenient."

"Who else knows of the notebook's existence, Madame?"

"No one but Isabelle, you, and myself. As for Phoebe's secret—she can be relied upon to keep it, though she is a little goose. She is convinced that her chances of making a brilliant match depend upon it and that the earl will no longer love her if he thinks she has not told the truth."

"I wonder who told her about the wager."

Madame shrugged. "It is not important. She knows. And she is afraid that your uncle will not marry her."

"He is besotted with her, Madame Zazou." Nigel sighed. "Though I do not hold Miss Sharpe in high regard myself. However, I am afraid he will do himself fatal harm if he feels obliged to defend her honor."

Ah—so that was why Nigel had come to Clarges

Street and stood beneath the window. He had wanted to speak to Madame but he happened to have seen Isabelle first—and flirted with her a little. Well, it was spring and that was nothing out of the ordinary. A man might flirt with a maid if it pleased him and it did not mean much. Isabelle's heart sank.

Madame nodded. "He is old and too often alone."

"Something like that." Nigel looked at Isabelle, wondering what she thought of all this. Phoebe had undoubtedly been rude to her, assuming in her petty way that Isabelle earned her own bread and was therefore unworthy of courtesy.

"You do understand, Mr. Wollaston, that we are in this together." She turned to Robert. "And you also must keep this secret."

"Yes, Madame." The boy seemed hurt that she would think otherwise.

"So—our forays against the enemy shall be made with stealth and swiftness. I have no wish to be notorious, and I will be if a hue and cry is raised in the street. Discretion is of the utmost importance in my business and privacy must be preserved at all costs."

"I understand perfectly," Nigel said.

"You know who some of these fellows are and something about their habits. I myself cannot hire an investigator or a Bow Street runner without attracting undue attention."

Nigel thought for a moment. "Most likely the culprits are George Sheridan or William Browne. They stand to gain the most."

"And we have much to lose. Now—Isabelle, if you would prepare Mr. Wollaston's bed, I would be grateful. Robert can help you carry things and perhaps build a fire. The room may be chilly, though it is spring."

The boy's face lit up. "I can do it, Madame. I have seen the cook set a fire in the kitchen many times."

Madame made a wry face. "Yes, she is over-generous with the cooking oil and careless with the dishcloths. It is a wonder she has not burned the house down."

"But she has showed me how, really she has. I will be very careful," he promised solemnly.

"Very good. Mr. Wollaston, Isabelle will see to your other needs."

Nigel gave Isabelle a broad smile. He seemed to be delighted by the plan, though she had her misgivings. Perhaps it was all a great adventure to him—but her feelings were hurt and her pride was pricked. And she dreaded being woken in the night by robbers or worse.

"Very well, Madame. Robert and I will prepare the room as you suggest."

They said good-night, and Isabelle collected linens and blankets from a closet in the upstairs hall on the way. Then Robert lit a candle and led them down the back stairs, through a dim corridor to a closed door she had never noticed.

"Our Sukey says the room is haunted, but 'tis only the coachman's old coat hanging from a peg that makes it seem so."

"Now, Robert," said Isabelle. "Sukey is just come from the country and every little thing frightens her."

The boy turned the doorknob, which let out a rusty creak. He handed the candle to Nigel.

"Do not be afraid, sir," he said reassuringly.

"My life is in your hands, my lad," Nigel replied solemnly.

The boy grinned. "Do you know, I once put on that old coachman's coat and pulled the collar over my head to chase Sukey. She screamed bloody murder. I should like to do it again."

"You must not," Isabelle said reprovingly. "I would scream, too, if a shapeless thing with no face chased me down a dark corridor."

Robert thought for a moment. "But I would not do that to you, Miss Mousey. And if someone hurt you, I would chop 'em to bits and pull out their guts."

"Quite right," said Nigel heartily. Miss Mousey was looking a little nervous and the dark corridor was no place to be talking about ghosts and guts. "And now—shall we enter?"

After a suitably dramatic pause, Robert swung the door inward. The room held no sign of life, supernatural or otherwise.

It did hold a bed or what passed for one: a rickety affair of poles and woven rope, with a tattered mattress. Nothing like the colossally comfortable four-poster of his recent fantasy, he noted with an inward smile. At least it was long enough. If he had to play the part of a coachman, he ought to be able to stretch out.

He looked around and opened the closet door as Isabelle and Robert began to make up the bed. There was nothing inside, and, as the boy had said, the old greatcoat hung from a peg outside it.

Nigel turned to see Isabelle and Robert shaking out a sheet. It billowed up and settled softly down, as they maintained a firm grasp on each of its four corners.

Isabelle smoothed the wrinkles from it. Watching her graceful arms and slender hands move over the plain sheets, making his bed with tender care, was an unexpectedly appealing sight.

She took a pillow from the table, stuffing it into a threadbare but clean pillowcase edged with crocheted lace—not Madame's finest linen, certainly, but serviceable—then set it aside.

Robert took another folded sheet and held out its edge to Isabelle, and they shook it out as they had the first, adding several blankets and putting more pillows into cases.

"I suppose there is no need for a fire," he said affably, watching them work.

She did not reply but pulled another candle from her pocket—clearly, she was thinking of his comfort, which was very nice of her—and set it beside the one he had just placed in the candlestick on the small table next to the bed.

"There. Is there anything else you might require, my lord?" Her teasing tone held a slight edge. She spoke as if they were equals, as if she, too, were only playing a part—but what that might be, Nigel had yet to discover.

He could not ask Madame about her charming assistant—not yet. And he was not supposed to speak to the other women he might encounter in the house in the next hours unless he had to. "Miss Mousey, if you would be so good as to show me through the house"—he paused and took a deep breath—"I should know where all the doors and windows are—and where everyone sleeps. In case there is an intruder."

Isabelle shot him a narrow look. "Of course."

Nigel scarcely knew what to say next, though he was perishing of curiosity.

Isabelle was clearly not a servant, yet she had been assigned the task of making his bed. She was obviously someone Madame trusted, yet she did not have the oppressed air or shabby clothes of a paid companion. She was young, she was beautiful, she was spirited, she was a gentlewoman, and she did not belong here. Yet she *was* here. Nigel was more puzzled than ever.

"My room is above yours. Madame's room is one door down from mine."

"I see."

"But I cannot lead you through the house. The maids might return soon."

"I will show you where I sleep. It is near the back door"—Robert took him by the hand—"and under another staircase that Miss Mousey did not mention—you cannot see it from here. But it leads to their rooms on the second floor."

Nigel let himself be led from the coachman's room, and Isabelle followed, closing the door behind her. Robert pointed out a neat little bed fitted upon planks under the stair risers. It was just big enough for a boy.

"The stairs creak most awfully when Fig sneaks out of Madame's room. He likes to sleep with me if he can."

Nigel put a foot upon the first stair to test it. It did indeed creak most awfully. He slid his foot two inches to the left. It creaked again, rather more loudly. He stepped upon the next one with his full weight. It creaked as well.

He nodded thoughtfully and stepped back down,

carefully but creakily, and spoke to Robert in a man-to-man way.

"Excellent. Miss Mousey and Madame Zazou will be safe."

"Of course—with us to guard them," Robert said importantly.

"If an intruder should get past Gabriel or Alf, and come this way, he will be caught by the creaks, Fig will sound the alarm throughout the house, and we shall overpower him."

"Can I wear the coachman's greatcoat?" Robert asked excitedly. "Let me show you how I look in it—" He dashed back into the room to get it, banging open the door.

Isabelle raised an elegant eyebrow. "Hm. The fox is set to guard the chickens, is that it?"

"You have nothing to fear from me, Miss Mousey. Creaking stairs are an inexpensive and effective guard of maidenly virtue. Ask any anxious papa—" He stopped, wondering again if she had one, or an anxious mama, for that matter. Surely her parents must not be alive.

"Boo!" Robert reappeared, or rather the great-coat with Robert inside it, his head and hands concealed within its voluminous length, reappeared. Nigel flinched. The headless, handless figure was enough to give anyone a start.

"Oh, Robert. Take it off. Sukey will run crying to Madame if she catches sight of you," Isabelle said patiently.

The boy's tousled head popped out. "Did I frighten you?" He wiped his nose upon the worsted-wool sleeve and grinned from ear to ear.

"Not in the least," Nigel lied. "Now put it back and run along."

The boy did as he was told. Nigel turned to escort Miss Mousey from the corridor.

Her expression was unfathomable. She cast her eyes down and kept her distance, though she followed him. Perhaps she *wanted* him to make some attempt upon her virtue—steal a kiss or something equally minor. Perhaps not. There was no reading her thoughts and Nigel found that most vexing of all.

# CHAPTER 14

*A shadow at the window . . .*

Isabelle closed the door to her room and flung herself on the bed.

Her emotions were best kept to herself. She did not want to admit her tender but mistaken feelings for Nigel Wollaston to anyone.

She would seem utterly foolish if she did. He had come to Madame Zazou's not to see her but to help his uncle—she had imagined those adoring looks and all the rest simply because she found him handsome. He was actually going to help silly, selfish Phoebe, whom Isabelle despised—oh, her thoughts were going in circles.

Worst of all, he would be *here* for a few days, at Madame's request. Isabelle could not simply ignore him and wait for her inconvenient infatuation to pass. Not when he would now be sleeping in the room below hers, though admittedly in a much less pleasant bed.

The thought made her want to howl with frustration.

She had to admit, if only to herself, that she would not mind if the stairs did creak underneath his manly footstep in the night. One kiss was all she would allow—one kiss, just to know what it felt like.

It was only a fantasy . . . and there was no harm in a fantasy, was there? But what if it did happen—how Fig would bark. She mentally banished Fig to the third floor for the duration of Mr. Wollaston's stay, where the little dog would not hear a thing.

She could defend her maidenly virtue with the fireplace poker, if it came to that, but one kiss from the oh-so-dashing Nigel would not ruin her forever. If he even wanted to kiss her, which she doubted. But Isabelle knew without question that she most certainly wanted to kiss *him*.

She would not sleep well tonight.

But she did sleep—and several hours later, Isabelle awoke. She had heard a noise—or had she been merely dreaming? *Thump*. No—there it was again. But it seemed to be coming from outside her window.

Her heart stopped beating when a shadow fell across the pane. She saw the outline of a man's arm and hand reaching toward the bottom of the window frame as if to open it. Isabelle opened her mouth to scream, then shut it.

Better to stop the intruder somehow before he entered—or to quietly summon help. She threw back the covers and rose from her warm bed, moving along the wall to the side of the window, almost noiseless, her feet bare on the cold floor. The shadow suddenly disappeared.

She waited, wondering what to do next. Then she heard a creak, then another, as rapid footsteps came near—and Nigel burst into her room. He wore nothing but flannel drawers and a loose open shirt that left his chest bare.

Isabelle averted her eyes. This was no time to be thinking about anything but the danger at hand.

He put a finger to his lips and moved along the wall toward her, grabbing her suddenly in one strong arm and putting her behind him. She saw a weapon in his hand—a piece of iron—perhaps it was a poker.

The shadow returned—it was now the outline of a man, and nearly covered the window. She saw the intruder balance and then bend, reaching with both hands for the bottom of the frame.

His fingers curled around it and he lifted it up noiselessly.

Nigel, pressing his back against the wall, motioned to her to be still. She stayed exactly where she was, realizing without caring that her tangled nightgown was well above her knees and revealed most of her thighs.

The intruder set one foot atop her small desk just under the windowsill, then the other, and crept inside, crouching upon the desk's top and breathing a little heavily as he peered around. Before he could jump to the floor, Nigel caught him a glancing blow on the side of the head.

The intruder groaned and fell off the desk, face down. Nigel dragged him by the collar into what little light there was and turned the unconscious man over.

"It is Sheridan!"

Isabelle simply stared, trembling now with fright. He straightened and took her in his arms until she was somewhat calmer. The man groaned again.

"Your friend?" she whispered.

He let go of her and returned to the man on the floor. "Not quite. But we know each other. He was in on the bet at White's and no doubt he hoped to win it. He has gambled away a fortune in the last month and most of it was his wife's dowry."

"Then I feel sorry for her."

"Everyone does. I should thrash him within an inch of his life. But he reeks of gin. He is undoubtedly drunk."

The man stirred slightly but did not open his eyes.

"Be careful, Nigel," she whispered nervously. "What if there is someone else outside?"

"There must be," Nigel whispered back. "Someone who brought a long ladder and held it for him. How else could he have climbed so high?"

Isabelle stole over to the window and looked out to see—only a ladder, leaning crookedly against the wall. There was no sign of anyone in the street.

"Look." She motioned him over to the window. But Nigel was busy. He had picked up one of her stockings to bind the intruder's wrists and tied his feet together with the other stocking. He ran a hand over the man's forehead, looking at his fingertips for blood. There was none.

"He has a goose-egg. Nothing more."

She had to admire his presence of mind. He had seemed to her too well-bred to be capable of such daring—and however had he learned to truss an intruder as neatly as that?

Nigel rose and picked up the piece of iron—it

was a fireplace poker, but a broken one that had been consigned to the coachman's room—and went to the window. His bare chest rose and fell with every breath he took, a wondrous sight to Isabelle, whose knowledge of masculine bodies had been heretofore confined to discreet peeks at statues.

He was magnificent. Almost indecently so. She wanted to fling her arms around him but she could not. They were alone in compromising circumstances, unless an unconscious man tied hand and foot counted as a chaperone. Thinking of the intruder brought her back to her senses.

"Oh, Nigel—whatever shall we do? We must wake Madame—"

He looked out the window, and up and down the street, seeing no one.

"Not yet. We may count ourselves lucky that Fig stayed in her room tonight, or the entire household would be in an uproar."

Isabelle nodded.

"Well, Mrs. Sheridan will find an unexpected parcel upon her doorstep in the morning. Let her deal with her bloody great fool of a husband."

"But I cannot lift him."

"Alf and Gabriel will help me. I will go out to the stables for Alf, and you must contrive to rouse Gabriel without waking the rest of the servants."

"The housemaids sleep in the attic and the kitchen servants sleep in the basement. He is the last one in at night and he locks the doors when all have retired."

Nigel nodded. "Then fetch him, and quickly. I will stay here, in case Sheridan opens his eyes or makes any sound. As Madame has asked, we shall keep this quiet."

Isabelle looked at him with round eyes.

"But she is right behind you."

Nigel whirled around.

"The deed is done," Madame Zazou said simply. "Someone has stolen the notebook."

"Oh no! But how did they get past Fig? Surely he would have barked—"

"He was not with me."

Nigel and Isabelle looked at each other.

"He was not with Robert." Nigel said. "I am sure of it, Madame. I passed his bed when I went up the stairs to Isabelle's room. I heard her feet upon the floor above me and I suspected trouble, so I grabbed the poker and took the stairs two at a time."

Madame looked coldly at the unconscious man upon the floor. "Get rid of him. I assume you know where he lives."

Nigel nodded.

"Isabelle, come with me. You are shaking. I will make you a soothing tisane."

"But Madame, where is Fig?"

She shrugged. "He got out somehow, I suppose. Perhaps he has found himself a lady friend. After all, it is spring—the season of fools."


Nigel did not show up at breakfast, and Madame Zazou looked thoughtfully at the dark circles under Isabelle's eyes.

"You did not sleep, *chérie?*"

"Ah—no."

"That is understandable, after what happened last night. I did not sleep myself. But at least I slept alone. Tell me, did Mr. Wollaston get rid of our unexpected guest?" the Frenchwoman inquired.

"I—I do not know, Madame. The man was not there when I returned to my room. And neither was Mr. Wollaston," she added hastily. Isabelle avoided the searching gaze of the woman across the table, briskly buttering her bread and stuffing it into her mouth to avoid answering further questions.

"You seem to be enjoying your breakfast. There are crumbs everywhere."

"Mm-hmf."

Madame folded her napkin, looked at Isabelle with faint disgust, and rose to leave.

Isabelle washed down the mouthful of buttered bread with a sip of café au lait from the small porcelain bowl Madame had set in front of her. She felt ever so slightly better and sipped more of the hot drink.

The door that had closed so firmly behind Madame opened again—and Nigel walked in. She smiled, though she had not quite wanted to. But somehow, seeing him there erased the last vestige of the terror she had felt, as if Nigel's mere presence might keep her safe from all harm.

Ridiculous.

Her mind clouded by sleepiness, she told herself that it was partly his fault all this was happening, because it was his uncle's fault—no, perhaps only Phoebe was to blame. There, she liked that explanation the best of all.

Isabelle hurriedly closed the rose-pink morning robe she wore over her nightgown and ran a hand over her uncombed hair. She had hoped to escape before he woke up, not wishing him to see her *en deshabille*—

"I have seen you in less, Miss Mousey," he said,

as if reading her mind. "Only last night, if you remember—"

"Of course I remember. Thank you for rescuing
me, by the way. I should have run to you immediately but I did not."

"At least you let me hit him with the poker," he
said nonchalantly.

"Yes—you stunned him quite nicely. What did
you do with Mr. Sheridan?"

Nigel yawned. "We untied him and left him upon
the front step of his house. Then we rang the bell
and the butler came out to drag him inside. He did
not seem in the least surprised. As I said, Sheridan
is over fond of drink. His loving wife may mete out
whatever punishment she sees fit."

"Did you tell her anything?"

"No. Madame Zazou wishes to avoid the least
breath of scandal and so do I. He did not succeed
in his quest and the bet will not be won."

"The notebook is gone, Mr. Wollaston."

"Am I Mr. Wollaston again? You called me Nigel
last night and fell into my arms. I rather liked it."

He went to the sideboard and lifted the lid of a
chafing dish, taking up a fork to poke at the fishy
concoction within. "Creamed kippers. Ugh. Is there
bacon?" He replaced the lid and lifted up another.
"Ah. Here it is." He picked out a crisp piece and
chewed it thoughtfully.

"Never mind the creamed kippers. I was in a
state of utmost agitation, you know."

"Well, you may still call me Nigel. If we have seen
each other in a state of undress, we might as well
use each other's first names from now on." Nigel
took a slice of toast from the silver toast rack and
spread it with jelly. "In any case, there was nothing

improper in my conduct and you cannot take me to task for protecting you." He munched his toast and studied her as he did so.

If only he would sit down—or better yet, go away. Isabelle squirmed inside her morning robe. Truly, every inch of her was completely covered and her person showed less than in some of her dresses. But she felt . . . bare.

"Why are you looking at me like that?"

Nigel grinned wickedly. "Tell me, Miss Mousey— how did you like being in my arms?"

"Oh! I will not answer that question!" She had liked being in his arms very much, of course. But to have him ask about it so forthrightly was most disconcerting.

"Very well." He sat down at last and cast a glance at the newspaper, which someone in the kitchen had ironed but not well. The ink was not yet dry. He opened it with a flourish and squinted at the narrow columns of type. "The news is never good."

Isabelle supposed that she was about to hear it anyway.

"There has been an earthquake in the South Seas—but that was months ago," Nigel began. "And I see that Napoleon is making a nuisance of himself in Austerlitz. And there is a Pageant of Vegetables at Covent Garden today. The most imposing cabbage will receive a ribbon from the Lord Mayor."

"There are no cabbages in spring. They are an autumn vegetable."

He shot her a look. "Ah. I stand corrected. So you are conversant with cabbages. Did you grow up in the country?"

She stuck another piece of buttered bread in her mouth. "Mm."

The mood was oddly domestic, as if they were a happy husband and contented wife, beginning their day together. She would hate to admit how much she liked it, though she did not like his inquisitiveness.

But she did not have to answer.

He rustled the pages of the newspaper, looking for something. He found it.

"Ah, here we are." He read silently for a minute. "That fearless critic, Mr. Poison Penn, says *Unguarded Intimacy* is the best play of the spring season. How unlike him to enjoy anything—he usually despises all but Shakespeare."

He scratched the faint stubble along his jaw and read aloud from the review. "*'Run, do not walk*—et cetera—*to Drury Lane and see it now.'* Would you accompany me, Isabelle?"

She shook her head. This particular occasion of unguarded intimacy was more than she could handle and certainly improper.

"Signora Giovanna Scrivani is dancing at the Royal Opera House," Nigel went on. "But Mr. Penn sniffs at her solo as a *Dying Swan*. Says she looks more like a dying mackerel flopping about."

Isabelle raised an eyebrow and sipped her coffee. "I am glad indeed not to be on stage with critics like that in the audience."

"No one takes him seriously or there would be no theatre-going in London. Truly, there is something for every taste. *Scarlet Women*—a melodrama. *The Pot That Call'd The Kettle Black*—a comedy. And there is *Love's Tiny Whiskers*—something about kittens, I believe."

"I have never seen a play about kittens." She had

never seen any play, as Lady Griselda routinely condemned theatres and theatre folk as immoral.

He folded the paper. "Mr. Penn does not recommend it."

"Then we shall not go. But thank you for the invitation. You are most kind."

Would Madame never return? Thank goodness the servants left everyone to their own devices before twelve o'clock. No one need know that he was here with her.

Nigel yawned again and stretched, blinking at the bright light through the windowpane before he set the paper aside.

Having shared many a breakfast with a great-aunt bedecked in curl papers and encrusted with improving facial creams, Isabelle had developed the habit of not looking up at that meal.

But she could not take her eyes from Nigel. His drowsy expression and sleepy, amiable smile were deliciously attractive.

It occurred to Isabelle that all couples should be required to share a breakfast table before marriage. The gentler illumination of candles and moonlight was famously untruthful, though certainly more romantic than the morning sun.

Yet she felt an inexpressible fondness for him just as he was now.

Nigel had not bothered to comb his hair either, or change. He had tossed a dressing gown, filched from somewhere, over what he had slept in just as she had. It did not fit him, being at least three inches too short in the sleeves, and it seemed comically abbreviated upon his long frame, as the hem was above his knees.

He resumed munching his jelly-laden toast, then peered into the coffee pot to see if any was left. There was none. He sighed deeply, looking enviously at hers.

Isabelle took a long sip, peering at him over the rim of the porcelain bowl. Perhaps Madame would return with fresh coffee before politeness obliged her to go fetch it.

She had decided to forgive him for not having been solely and exclusively interested in her at first. After all, if fate had thrown them together, she could not argue with fate. And if he had his uncle's interests at heart, that was as good an indication of a kind nature as one might wish.

Nigel studied her, trying to read her thoughts. How was it possible that she could look so pretty in the morning? He had never known a woman who would even let him glance in her direction before noon.

Isabelle's pure complexion showed not a trace of paint or powder, and her splendid honey-colored hair was unconfined by a mobcap or ribbon.

All he had to do was reach across the table to touch it, draw its silken richness through his hand before he stroked her soft cheek and—hang it. He needed coffee very badly indeed.

The warmth of the sun was making him stupid. Was he to have nothing more than the fragrance of the stimulating drink he craved?

He set down his crust and stood up, walking to a bellpull hanging near the door. "Does this work in the fashion of the one in the dining room? I wish to summon the cook."

"Yes, it works. But the servants should not see us like this."

"Well, then I will hide under the table when they come."

She giggled. "The bell system is different in the morning, you know."

"Then explain it, if you would be so kind," he said irritably.

She set down her bowl and licked a slight trace of milky coffee from her upper lip in a most provocative and annoying way. Nigel glared at her.

"Ring once for tea, twice for coffee. Three for toast, and four for kippers. Five long rings for eggs, followed by one short ring for soft-boiled and two longs for poached. Six rings for—"

"I suppose bacon is six and marmalade seven," Nigel grumbled.

"Try it and see," she said cheerfully. "I do not remember the higher numbers."

He rang twice and went back to wherever it was he had come from. In due time, the cook bustled in and refilled the coffee pot.

"There you are, miss—but you have plenty of coffee. Are you alone? Where is Madame Zazou?"

That lady rustled into the room, almost as if she had been listening on the other side of the door. The cook left, and Nigel walked back in.

"Ah—our hero. *Bonjour, m'sieu!*" She brushed a kiss on both of his stubbly cheeks and patted him on the back.

"Good morning, Madame Zazou." Nigel threw Isabelle a self-satisfied look, as if to say *now that is how a hero should be treated,* and sat down to his coffee.

# CHAPTER 15

*The language of flowers . . .*

Shortly after breakfast, when she had made herself presentable, Isabelle went to see Jehane in her chamber on the top floor. She looked forward to this task: filling windowboxes and any container the cook would not miss with primroses and pansies and so forth.

The old lady had sent for Isabelle the moment she heard the cry of the man who sold potted plants from his wooden cart and soft, peaty earth in burlap bags.

Robert had brought up the heavy bags of dirt one by one and earned himself an extra shilling from Madame for his labors on behalf of her mother. Isabelle spread a piece of drugget over the carpet by the window, and the two gardeners set to work.

Jehane wore gloves so as not to roughen her fingertips, which might then snag on the fine threads she worked with. But Isabelle dug her bare hands into the bags of dirt, enjoying its loamy smell and dark richness.

She had been a great one for roaming the copses and hedgerows around the Priory—one thing at least that she missed very much in London. Her excursions to Hyde Park with Robert were not at all the same. But she would return to Surrey at some point—Isabelle still did not know when.

*"Ma chère,"* Jehane said softly. "Cut this geranium here—and here." She indicated the spots with a finger, cradling the small plant in one hand. "Put in water for growing roots and we will have two plants—so."

The old lady was nothing if not thrifty. The cuttings she had asked Isabelle to take at the physick garden they had visited a few weeks ago were now flourishing upon the windowsill in blue-and-white earthenware pots. In fact, some of the plants were beginning to crawl up the walls and extend tendrils along the eaves, especially the ivy.

When told of this, Jehane had been delighted, hoping that birds might nest someday within this tangle of green when it was thick enough.

Isabelle had not minded a bit of horticultural larceny on the old lady's behalf in the physick garden. She had cut and clipped as directed—Jehane identified the plants she wanted by crushing the leaves Isabelle plucked between her forefinger and thumb.

She had concealed the sprigs in her reticule and even stuck a few into the ribbon of her bonnet, avoiding the suspicious gaze of the head gardener as they left.

Jehane sighed with pleasure, scrabbling a hole

in the dirt for her beloved forget-me-nots. Or *yeux de Marie*, as she called them. Mary's eyes. The old lady was a devout Catholic and often prayed her beads kneeling upon a worn velvet stool, Isabelle knew. Madame herself seemed to have no particular faith beyond kindness to her fellow man.

And woman, Isabelle amended, thinking again of how Madame had taken her in so trustingly. She would never betray that trust.

She saw Jehane lift her head suddenly and stop her work, listening. Isabelle heard nothing—no sparrow, no starling—only the faintest rustle of leaves somewhere below.

The old lady turned to Isabelle as if she could see her and beckoned her to the window. Isabelle quickly reached her side and looked down into the small garden and then to the mews, following Jehane's pointing finger.

She saw nothing.

"I heard steps. There is a man below. Not Alf. Not Gabriel. I know their sounds."

Isabelle looked again. A clump of shrubbery near the back door stirred ever so slightly. The door had been carelessly left open—but she reminded herself that not everyone knew of the precautions Madame was taking. Madame had undoubtedly told her mother, however.

She saw a man's hat, much crushed and dirty, rise through the shrubbery, but she could not see the man's face.

At that moment, Alf came out of the stable and saw him too. "Hoi! You there! Stop, thief!"

The man moved left and then right, unsure of which way to turn and obviously afraid of the strapping Alf.

Isabelle brushed past Jehane to pick up a large pot overflowing with pansies, but the old lady put a hand on her arm when she heard the pot scrape against the windowsill and Isabelle's indrawn breath from the effort of lifting it. "No! We must capture him alive and find out who does this to us!"

"I only mean to dump the dirt on his head, Jehane!" Isabelle quickly tipped the pot over the windowsill, holding firmly to its rim, and did just that.

Her aim was true. The man coughed and spluttered, brushing dirt from his eyes and a pansy from his mouth.

Alf ran forward and threw his brawny arms around the man's chest and wrestled him to the ground, sitting on him triumphantly. "Well done, Miss Mousey and Madame Jehane! Thought ye were going to knock his brains out with that flower pot, I did!"

Sukey, the scullery maid, came out into the garden with a bucket of dishwater and dashed it on the flagstones. "Who is *that*—is he hurt?"

"He will be if he isn't yet. Back to the kitchen, my girl."

She scuttered inside.


The coachman's old bedroom was crowded with three big men—Alf, Gabriel, and Nigel—and one small dog—Fig. All were glowering at a surly, young-ish fellow who had just handed over Madame's precious notebook.

Nigel riffled through the pages, which appeared

to have been written in some kind of code. None were torn out, though he supposed it might have been copied.

"Who put you up to this, man?" Nigel demanded.

"I was told to return that. And I have done. Let me go," the fellow said.

"What is your name? And who are you working for?"

"I have no name," he muttered sullenly.

Alf and Gabriel simultaneously clenched their fists. "No name—we'll give ye no name, lad!"

Not to be outdone, Fig seized the man by the ankle and gnawed at his heavy boot, to no avail.

"Call off your dog!" No Name shouted. He shot out a foot to kick the little animal and was immediately and soundly cuffed for it by Alf.

"Ow!"

"More where that came from," Alf said pleasantly.

"All right then. Willy Browne gave me a half-crown and that little book. He said I was to leave it inside this house, anywhere—like someone had dropped it. I was just about to do it when I was rudely interrupted by a pot of pansies."

"None o' yer repartee, lad," growled Gabriel.

"Can I go? You have the book. You know who sent me."

The three men exchanged considering looks. Nigel nodded.

"Yes—go. But if Alf or Gabriel sees your face within a mile of Clarges Street, they will smash it in. Is that perfectly clear?"

He nodded, rubbing his ear.

"Alf, show him out."

The coachman did as he was bid, but none too gently. No Name took to his heels when he reached the open street and was soon lost to view.


Nigel handed the little notebook to Madame, who riffled through its pages carefully. *"Bien.* It is intact."

He shook his head. "It could have been copied. You did not tell me it was in code, Madame."

She shrugged. "Truly, I never thought it would be stolen—no one knows what is in it but myself. But perhaps someone within the house has guessed well. Someone who has seen me writing in it and knew where I kept it, if nothing else."

"Perhaps." He waited for her to suggest a suspect but she did not. "Your mother has marvelous powers of hearing. She noticed the man before anyone else."

"Yes. I am glad that Isabelle was with her—not that I ever leave Maman alone. She is more frail than ever."

Nigel almost envied her, reminded at that moment of the mother he had lost so early in life. "Yet you are lucky to have her with you, Madame."

"I know."

A brief silence fell until Madame returned to the subject of the notebook.

"Well—you have said that William Browne is a fool. He will not understand a code of my own invention."

It was Nigel's turn to shrug. "Perhaps he intends to pay someone to translate it for him. The bet is still on. There is one more day."

Madame sighed irritably. "This is such a—how do you English say it? A temptress in a teapot. Poor Phoebe."

Nigel hid a smile with a polite cough. "The phrase is 'tempest in a teapot,' I believe. Now should we tell poor Phoebe of this or not?"

Madame Zazou pondered the question for several seconds. "I think not. We have the notebook. And no one will figure out my code. It is the gutter French of Paris, something like your Cockney, with a number to replace each vowel—and it is written backwards."

Nigel raised an eyebrow. "I am surprised that *you* could keep track of it, Madame."

"Do you know, I think Sukey must have led our burglar to it. She is the only one in the house who cannot read and she would not have known that it was in code. She must be sacked and soon."

Nigel nodded. That was the girl who had been persuaded to talk for a sixpence. "Still, unless Browne knows an expert on such things at the Admiralty, we are probably safe enough."

"*Pah*, the Admiralty," Madame sniffed. "Old sailors, pickled in rum and decorated with gold braid. And please do not inquire as to what I think of the Army."

Nigel was not about to ask what a woman of her experience knew about sailors and soldiers. "Perhaps I should introduce you to my uncle, the exceedingly distinguished earl," he said jovially. "Not a bit of gold braid on him, though he has served his King and country well for many years."

Madame looked at him very thoughtfully and shrugged. "I should like to meet him—why not?"

"Ah—yes," said Nigel. He had not expected her to take his remark seriously at all. But she had— and he could not now be rude to her.

"I have it! We shall give another dinner party to celebrate the notebook's return and invite the most amusing people we know. Do you think he would attend?"

"Ah—of course. Dear old Bertie loves amusing people." Which was true enough—and his uncle was not a snob when it came to enjoying himself. Besides, Nigel was suddenly intrigued by the idea of his uncle meeting the beautiful Miss Mousey.

Perhaps the old earl would know someone who knew her, or even just knew of her. Whatever information Nigel might glean on this subject would be welcome. Bertie had been long a leader in society, despite his absences abroad, and his connections were extensive.

And speaking of connections—"May I invite my friend, Jeremy Gresham, the writer?"

Madame nodded eagerly. "I have heard of him! Who has not? He is the writer, the publisher, the scandalmonger, the ugly lover of so many women— is he not enamored of Mrs. Baddeley?"

"Grace Baddeley—yes."

Madame was too discreet to mention that Grace was one of her clients, Nigel noted with approval. "Shall I invite her as well, Madame? She loves to talk. It will be a lively affair."

"Those are the best kind, *m'sieu!*" After that exclamation, Madame sat for a moment, lost in thoughts she seemed to have no intention of sharing. "Well, I will leave it to you and Isabelle to plan the details. She is a capable young woman and I have much work to do today."

"Very well—it will be my pleasure. But one question remains—where will you keep the book now?"

She tapped the side of her head. "In here. I will remember what is important. I shall burn it today. There will be no more bets made at my expense." She looked through the little book once more and set it aside with a sigh.

Nigel bowed and withdrew, and went in search of Isabelle.

He thought to wash up a bit first and managed a passable shave with Alf's razor. The coachman was kind enough to strop it for him to an acceptable sharpness and Nigel had not even nicked himself. He doubted that Isabelle would plant any kisses on his newly smooth face if they were to ride in an open carriage, but a man could hope.

Glimpsed only by a busy housemaid, who nodded casually as if the sight of a man about the house was nothing at all unusual, Nigel searched and found Isabelle at last on the top floor, in Jehane's chamber. The door was open and he was for a moment a silent witness to a charming scene: Isabelle was reading from the essays of Montaigne— in excellent French, he noted—but the old lady had fallen asleep with Fig on her lap. The dog was curled up tightly, nose to tail, his eyes half-open.

Both of them looked up when they saw him enter, but Fig did not jump from Jehane's lap. Isabelle softly closed the book. "I am waiting for her lady's-maid—ah, here is Louisette."

A shy young girl stood just outside the door and Isabelle gestured to her to enter. She dropped a bumbling curtsy to Nigel and Isabelle said something to her very quietly in French to explain his presence.

The girl nodded, not seeming to care one way or another. She looked about for her knitting, picked it up, and resumed the manufacture of an extraordinarily long stocking.

Fig watched the clicking needles with interest, his eyes moving to and fro with their rhythm, but he remained where he was on the old lady's lap.

*"Bien,"* said Isabelle, rising. She walked with him to the door and closed it quietly behind them.

Nigel smiled down upon her. "For a moment you sounded exactly like Madame."

Isabelle raised an eyebrow. "Well, that is no surprise, as we live together." She preceded him down the stairs, lifting her dress with one hand and sliding the other along the banister.

"And how long have you lived here, Isabelle, if I may ask?"

"You may ask, but I shan't answer," she said impudently.

"Very well. Then I shall not tell you where we are going. Madame said we might have the carriage all day, and Alf is at our service."

"Hm. Have any of the maids seen you? I suppose we must continue to be discreet, even though the notebook has been returned."

"Discretion is a very great virtue, Miss Mousey," Nigel said slyly. "But it is possible to be too discreet as well."

Whatever did he mean by that? Isabelle was

not sure she would want her question answered. Emboldened by the night he had spent under Madame's roof and the unexpectedly intimate breakfast they had shared, he seemed to be working up to making inquiries of a most personal nature.

She rounded the newel post on the next landing and picked up speed as they went down the subsequent flight of stairs.

Really, there seemed to be no end to this house, Nigel thought. There were small rooms everywhere and narrow halls that turned blind corners. A strange person clad from head to foot in black bombazine came rustling toward them, wearing large pointed shoes.

"Good day, Mrs. Shrinking," Isabelle said airily, a little out of breath. "Allow me to introduce Mr. Wollaston, a friend of Madame's—"

The lady in black muttered something and disappeared at the end of a corridor. Had she really said what he thought he heard—*none of your shifty looks?*

Madame's household was most irregular—but for now, he had to concentrate on keeping up with Miss Mousey.

"Are you not even curious as to our destination?"

"I will be able to see where we are going once we are in the carriage."

He took a deep breath upon the ground floor and realized that Isabelle had not answered the first question he had put to her. Would he never find out more about her? She seemed utterly determined to keep him at a distance.

She bestowed a charming smile upon Gabriel and collected her bonnet on the way out the door. Nigel gave him a nod. "Thank you again, Gabriel.

You are a veritable Cerberus when it comes to guarding this door."

Gabriel grinned. "Is that the big dog wif three heads as what guards the gates of Hades?"

"Yes—but how did you know?"

"Miss Mousey once said the same thing ye just did. Only she hexplained it and said it was a compliment, like. Well, enjoy yer outing, sir. It is a lovely day."

"Indeed it is." He stepped outside, lost in thought and rapidly adding up what he knew about her so far. Isabelle was well-educated indeed for a woman: she read Gibbon on the decline and fall of empires, spoke perfect French, and was versed in ancient myth. She knew when cabbages sprang forth from the earth and she knew her way around a flower-pot. Certainly it was possible she had been raised in the country, as he had tried to get her to admit this morning—but where?

Her manners were not quite sophisticated, but her natural charm more than made up for any minor lapses in conduct. She was independent and quick-witted, and she—

Isabelle was standing by the carriage, tapping her foot in its pretty shoe impatiently.

He finished his thought. And she did not like to wait. He wondered how he might turn that particular trait of her character to his own advantage, before he helped her up, under Alf's watchful eye.

"Where to, sir?"

"The Covent Garden market. And points east. We are going shopping. Madame has planned a dinner to celebrate the return of the notebook."

"I see," Isabelle said dryly. "And who are the guests, since she seems to have taken you into her confidence and not me?"

"It was her idea—an impulsive one. I will tell you all the details on the way. I expect it will be a most amusing evening."

# CHAPTER 16

*A secret client . . .*

They returned three hours later, rattling along Piccadilly laden with wonderful food—some prepared and some not—roses by the dozens in Madame's favorite deep red, and several bottles of excellent wine.

They stopped last at a confectioner's glass-fronted shop for sweets.

"Wait here, Nigel. I shall go in—you are half-buried in parcels."

She descended with assistance from Alf, who grinned at the sight of his lordship. "Robert ought to be 'elping ye. But Madame set him to blacking everyone's boots today."

"I don't mind in the least, Alf. Spending time with Miss Mousey is a very great pleasure."

The coachman laughed outright. "If ye say so, sir."

"What gentleman would not be happy to carry twice as much for her?"

Alf nodded. "I take yer meaning. And I have never seen her look so happy neither."

Isabelle exited the shop at that moment, a spring in her step and yet another parcel—a very small one, with licorice for Madame and Turkish delights for her guests—in her hand. Her cheeks were rosy and her hair almost tumbled down over her shoulders. She looked impossibly pretty.

Nigel wished he could hold her in his arms instead of unromantic things like filleted flounder and beefsteaks and lettuces, however nicely they were wrapped.

She tossed him the sweets in a carefree way and climbed in with a hand from Alf. "There. We have bought everything good to eat in London and taken the air as well. Let us go home. Dinner is at eight and we will not leave the house once it begins."

He thought for a moment. If he could get her alone—

"We might make an escape afterwards."

"How? Out the window and over the chimney-pots?"

"If you like. I have received several invitations to balls in the last few weeks—one might be tonight. Do you enjoy dancing, Miss Mousey?"

She grew wistful of a sudden, and he wished he had not asked. She did not reply immediately, looking away from him and out as Alf turned the carriage into the crowded street with some difficulty.

Dancing—if only she could. But that was one

thing the old professor had never taught her, the worthy scholar of humanities not knowing how himself.

Lady Griselda had thought dancing and dancing masters a shocking waste of time and money, but she acknowledged both as a social necessity. Thus, she had once—and only once—led Isabelle through a minuet at a pace suitable for a funeral procession and considered her duty done.

"I do not know how," Isabelle said at last. "And I do not go out in society. No one would invite a corsetière's assistant to a ball."

He studied her profile, wanting only to see the smile that had vanished so abruptly. "I suspect you are much more than that, though you reveal nothing about yourself. You would shine at the most brilliant assembly. If Madame might be persuaded to lend you the right clothes, you would be a diamond of the first water."

"Hm."

"Confide in me, dearest. Did you commit some indiscretion? Were you turned out from your home?"

"No. I cannot tell you more at the moment. But I will—I promise you that."

"Very well—I can ask for no more. Now if you would like to learn to dance—that is, if I might have the honor of teaching you, I would be— um—honored."

She turned and looked at him thoughtfully. Nigel was delighted to see her smile slowly return.

"Perhaps. We shall see. The waltz—that is what I would like to learn. I have heard it makes one dizzy in a most delightful way."

However much Lady Griselda disapproved of dancing, the old lady had thought waltzing positively decadent. Isabelle could not wait to try it.

Madame was at her desk, busy with various papers, but she looked up with a smile as Isabelle entered. "Did you and Nigel complete the shopping?"

"Yes. He has gone to his Albany Court apartments to change and the cook is already hard at work. We bought some prepared dishes so as to be ready and Turkish delights for a sweet."

Madame tapped her pencil on the desk. "Excellent. I am planning the seating. We shall put the earl next to Jeremy. I have heard that Bertram enjoys the company of eccentrics."

"Who told you that, Madame?" It struck her as odd that Madame referred to him by his first name, as if dining with earls were something she did every day. But perhaps that was the custom in France—Isabelle was not sure and thought it impolite to ask.

"Oh, Nigel may have mentioned it, I do not quite remember. Jeremy shall sit next to you—I have heard that he is a wicked little man, you will like him and he is certain to like you. I wonder what Nigel will think of that."

Again, Isabelle was taken aback by Madame's bluntness about who would sit where, a subject that was apt to give hostesses in polite society fainting fits. "I did not quite hear what you just said, Madame."

"I said that Jeremy is a wicked little man. Now, where to put his mistress? Grace Baddeley cannot sit above the salt—"

"Do you mean Mrs. Baddeley?" Isabelle inquired eagerly. "*The* Mrs. Baddeley? Your secret client?" Grace came and went from Madame's through a different door than the haughty Phoebe. She was reputed to be one of the most beautiful females in London but *the* Mrs. Baddeley was no more married than Isabelle was.

"The very same, though she has no need of an Invisible Arrangement, having a flawless figure. You may be sure it will be on display. The painter Moreville has often used her as a model in different guises."

"I have seen his *Venus Rising* at the Royal Academy exhibitions. Is that her?"

"Yes, Isabelle," Madame said patiently. "But she is a mortal woman, not a goddess, though *charmant* in her rustic way. We shall seat her below and beside the earl. Jeremy will not mind. I shall seat him next to you, as I said."

She bent over a little sketch she had drawn of the table, humming under her breath.

Isabelle would rather be next to Nigel but made no protest. She was beginning to believe that his feelings for her were real, but she did not want to encourage him.

Sooner or later she would be found out. Despite Isabelle's diligent attention to her misleading correspondence, Lady Griselda could not be deluded forever and might swoop down at any moment, embarrassing her and putting Madame in a most difficult position.

As for the alternative—confessing who she was and where she was from—Isabelle doubted that Nigel would want her once he learned of her deception, however harmless it had been. Strictly speaking, she had not lied but merely sidestepped some of his questions, unwilling to end her escapade or reveal her true identity.

Oh, her adventurous nature might well be her undoing—anyone would wonder why a well-bred girl would stay at Madame's house and her explanation was sure to raise more questions than it would answer.

As Lady Griselda had often told her, Isabelle had not a brass farthing she might call her own. Her worthy relation had also taken pains to point out again and again that her niece owed her a great debt for being allowed to live at the Priory for so long.

It was a wonder Griselda did not charge for the air she breathed, Isabelle thought—unlike Madame, who was always generous and had taken her in with scarcely a question asked.

Though Isabelle had somehow taken Nigel's fancy just as she was, modestly dressed in cast-off garb and making little of herself, that fancy was likely to be fleeting. True, they had spent the last twenty-fours in happy proximity, but once the excitement over the idiotic bet was over, he would go on his merry way.

Nigel Wollaston would eventually come to his senses and forget all about her. As the son of a second son, he was certainly expected to wed an heiress, not a penniless orphan—and it was presumptuous of her to even think about their time together as anything more than an amusing interlude in his life and her own. The thought was sobering.

Isabelle would have to marry for money herself—or accept the cold embrace of a twitchy curate. She hardly wished to follow the mercenary example of Miss Sharpe, but the world offered women very little choice. And that reminded her—

"By the bye, Madame, what about Miss Sharpe?"

Madame merely sniffed. "She considers herself too respectable to associate with a woman who is not received in society. The *ton* will hang paintings of Grace in her naked glory upon their walls, but they will not break bread with her. It would not be so in France."

Isabelle thought it over. "Perhaps it is to our advantage that Grace is not received."

"A shrewd observation, my dear Isabelle. Phoebe is sure to hear that her 'dear Bertie' dined with a famous beauty, but she will be unable to do anything about it. The little hypocrite is not likely to admit that she has ever heard of Mrs. Baddeley."

"You are right," replied Isabelle cheerfully.

Madame twiddled her pencil between her forefinger and thumb and her lips curved in a satisfied smile. "So—that is the guest list. One literary lion. One professional beauty. One handsome young man and his uncle. Myself. And you."

Isabelle added it up. "Three men and three women—that works out nicely and we shall not want for things to talk about."

"Make sure beeswax candles are used, Isabelle, not tallow, and instruct the maids to put fresh ones in the chandelier. And roses—roses everywhere! You did remember to buy roses, did you not?"

Isabelle nodded. "Mr. Wollaston insisted upon paying for them. They are a gift from him to you."

"He is a very kind man. Sometimes I cannot be sure, but—do you not like him a little, Isabelle?"

She hesitated. "More than a little, Madame."

* * *

The household was in a glorious uproar by the time they retreated to Madame's chamber to dress. She opened the door of a small adjoining room, which had been pressed into service as a closet.

"Pick one," Madame said, waving a hand at the rows of gowns.

It seemed an impossible task. The evening gowns hung from ceiling rods to accommodate their trains, and the day dresses hung below. The room was crammed with garments in a dizzying multitude of colors and styles, and the pungent smell of lavender sachets made Isabelle want to sneeze.

She rubbed her nose rather inelegantly and crossed the threshold. It was difficult to take a step or even to turn, as the dresses were everywhere. Some were not finished, she saw, awaiting a final fitting or perhaps simply left by customers who could not pay their bills.

Isabelle ran her hand over a rack at shoulder height—any might do, all were pretty.

Madame pulled a pale blue confection from its hanger and held it up to Isabelle. "*Non*. It is too— girlish. Something more sophisticated, perhaps." She resumed her search, humming happily.

"What will you wear, Madame?"

The Frenchwoman burrowed through the racks and brought forth a stunning dress in deep red charmeuse, with jet beading decorating the plunging neckline. "This."

Madame's dark hair and eyes would be set off beautifully by the rich color, Isabelle knew. But she wondered for a second or two who it was that Madame intended to dazzle, since no Venerable Admirers had been invited.

Perhaps the older women simply wanted to look her best. Certainly Isabelle did.

Madame was absorbed in considering the merits of other dresses for Isabelle. "*Non.* Too prim. *Non.* Too tight. *Non.* Too many feathers!" This last was a bright green horror that owed much to the ostrich. "*Zut*—it is no wonder the lady refused to pay for it. Ah—here is the one for you."

She selected a gown in cream-colored moiré, adorned with tiny ribbon roses and a matching sash. It was décolleté but not immodestly so. "Exactly right. It is virginal but also—not virginal—I cannot think of the right word. Your Nigel will not be able to take his eyes from you."

"He is not my Nigel, Madame." And never would be, most likely, Isabelle thought sadly.

"He is not? I have done everything in my power to bring you together as often as possible—and the look in his eyes is that of a man in love."

Isabelle opened her mouth to reply but no sound came out at first. What could she say? She had suspected more than once that Madame had left them alone together of a purpose, but these intervals had never been quite long enough to be improper.

"Do not thank me," Madame said graciously. "I find matchmaking quite amusing."

"I see." Isabelle had not known this. Madame seemed quite happy to remain independent herself.

The Frenchwoman exited the closet with both dresses in her arms, Isabelle behind her. "I myself prefer to keep my admirers at some distance— their demands can be exhausting. But you are young and ought to marry, *n'est-ce pas?* Why not Nigel?"

Why not indeed? Isabelle had no answer at the ready.

"Maman agrees with me. It is time. Women should not wait too long."

"But I have no fortune."

Madame set the dresses on the bed and patted Isabelle's cheek. "Your face is your fortune, *chérie*. Do not worry!"

# CHAPTER 17

*A surprising revelation . . .*

The guests gathered in the dining room, and Madame seated them according to her plan. Nigel seemed disappointed not to be next to Isabelle, but he turned to Mrs. Baddeley and engaged her in conversation immediately, much to Isabelle's annoyance.

Once the first few courses had been brought in and placed in the center of the long table, Madame dismissed the servants with a nod.

Jeremy nodded with approval. "Like the French aristocrats, eh? No ears to listen, no tales to tell."

"And no heads left on any of 'em," Bertie said affably.

Nigel and Isabelle looked at Madame simultaneously. If she was offended, she showed no sign of it.

"Ooh, soup," said Grace, lifting the lid of a majolica tureen in the shape of a resting cow and sniffing appreciatively.

Nigel suddenly remembered the chicken tureen, which had given up pride of place to this bovine usurper. Madame must have several—she seemed to like to entertain and if she preferred her guests to do the serving, he was happy to oblige. "Allow me to serve you, Mrs. Baddeley." He took up the ladle with a gentlemanly flourish.

Pricked by a sudden feeling of jealousy that she knew was unworthy, Isabelle sat in silence. She did approve of his lack of snobbery. If Nigel treated every woman, even the fabulously disreputable Mrs. Baddeley, like a lady, perhaps there was hope for her.

"Well, we will be quite comfortable without all the lads in livery, I expect." Jeremy leaned back slightly in his chair and gave Isabelle a measuring look. "What do you think, Miss Mousey?"

All eyes were upon her and she blushed deeply. "Oh—we shall get on without them, I suppose." In truth, she would have been grateful for the coming and going and the clatter of courses arriving and departing. She was used to being inconspicuous, and knew she was not in the beautiful cream-colored gown.

Nigel instinctively understood how uncomfortable Isabelle felt at the moment. He reflected again upon her essential innocence, despite her often forward ways. But all he could do was look at her inquiringly, the ladle still in his hand. "And what would you like, Miss Mousey?"

She would like to be anywhere else but here, she thought, feeling very awkward indeed. Her happy mood of the afternoon had evaporated somewhere between picking out the dress and the arrival of the guests, and she could not say quite why. "Nothing, thank you. Well, perhaps I will have a little wine to start." She hoped she would not spill it on her dress in her nervousness.

"Allow me," said Jeremy, picking up the decanter and filling her glass.

Nigel looked around, ready to serve the others. His uncle laughed. "I say, Nigel, you are a dab hand with a ladle. We shan't need servants at all."

Madame looked a touch put out. "I did not mean for your nephew to assume responsibility. I can summon help in an instant." She pointed to the bellpull. "One ring for the meat, two rings for the fish, three for bread and butter. And so on."

"Quite all right," Nigel said hastily. "My uncle was merely speaking in jest. Now—would you like to begin with beef bouillon, Bertie?" he asked, kicking the old earl under the table. "Or perhaps you would prefer the aspic."

"Ow! No! No broth, I mean," Bertie said hastily. "On my physician's advice, I have been drinking vats of it. Hasn't done a bit of good. But the aspic will not trouble my digestion."

Madame bestowed a pleased smile upon him. She looked regal, her rounded arms and snowy bosom set off elegantly by the dark red gown.

The old earl cast an appreciative eye upon her charms. Madame leaned forward ever so slightly to reveal a little more as she slid a trembling slice of aspic onto his plate.

Isabelle tried not to stare. Was Madame bent upon making a conquest of Nigel's uncle? The Frenchwoman would lose Phoebe as a customer if so, but she would gain ... another Venerable Admirer. Oho. So that was why she had taken such care in dressing.

This impromptu dinner was becoming more interesting by the minute. Isabelle drank deeply from her glass of wine and coughed a little, unused to the taste and the heady effect.

Grace Baddeley looked at Lord Wollaston, who was attacking his aspic. "I should like some of that. It wiggles very nicely."

"As do you, dearest," said Jeremy, draining his second glass of wine. He reached past Isabelle for the aspic. "Excuse me, Miss Mousey. Would you like some as well?"

She noticed he had accidentally dipped his cuff in the sauce. "No, thank you. I will begin with the bouillon after all." She lifted the lid from the tureen and took up the ladle that Nigel had set down.

Bowls and plates were passed and filled and handed round, and the meal began in earnest.

There were more cold courses than hot, owing to the decision to dine without servants, but that was just as well, for the evening was warm and the room rather stuffy.

Despite the ringing of the bellpull at the prescribed intervals, there was an overlong period between the removal of the meat course and the arrival of the fish. Madame excused herself to see to the preparation of the latter, still not trusting the cook.

Grace and Isabelle chatted animatedly with Jeremy, who was delighted to have the full attention of two such lovely women. He regaled them both with amusing stories and yet more wine—much more wine than was good for them, Nigel noted with disapproval.

His uncle had turned to more manly topics, the Wollaston practice hunt among them. This gathering had taken place as planned, and from his uncle's account, Nigel was glad he had not attended. He wondered what his father, Lord Charles, had thought of Phoebe, but he scarcely dared to ask.

After a tedious discussion of horses and hounds—and more than a few longing looks at Miss Mousey, who did not seem to notice them, Nigel was feeling somewhat out of sorts.

Was it because Isabelle was decidedly tipsy? Or was it because she was giggling at Jeremy's scandalous jokes? He could not say. The three of them were taking turns scribbling on a piece of paper the writer had pulled from his pocket.

Jeremy stood up, ready to declaim. "Ahem. I have it. *What muse inspires amorous rhyme? Why, two parts gin and one part lime!*" He sat down, laughing more uproariously than the ladies.

Nigel rose and repaired to the small balcony of the dining room with his uncle, knowing that Bertie wished to smoke, a habit he only indulged outside. They closed the French doors quietly behind them—not that the merrymakers seemed to appreciate their politeness or even notice that they had left the table, Nigel thought irritably.

From an inside pocket, Bertie withdrew a meerschaum pipe with a slender stem and a small bowl. He packed it with fragrant tobacco from a small pouch and lit it with the taper Nigel had pinched from the chandelier on the way out.

As the old earl drew his first puffs, Nigel watched a thin ribbon of smoke ascend to the night sky.

This was a ritual they had shared upon occasion since he had been very young, usually when one or the other of them wished to share some confidence.

"What were we talking about, Nigel?" his uncle asked between puffs.

"The Wollaston hunt."

"Oh, yes. It was a disaster, more or less. Your father was rude to Phoebe and we left as soon as we could. I did not want to tell the story in front of Jeremy. I suppose you amused yourself in town."

"Yes—if chasing burglars can be considered amusing."

"Burglars? What sort of company do you keep?"

"Madame Zazou, to whom I was introduced only very recently,"—Nigel did not want to explain how recently or Jeremy's part in it all at the moment— "requested that I stay at her house for a few days. She had seen a prowler."

"She is a charming woman, and most elegant. Soignée, as the French say. But why did she happen to ask you for help?"

"She thought the prowler might be—someone I knew."

"Really, Nigel, this cryptic conversation is most annoying. Will you not tell me what you were doing here and why? Is the lovely Madame Zazou a diamond smuggler or a spy?"

"No."

"Why did she invite me?"

Nigel shifted uncomfortably, having no immediate or logical answer to this question, as he had not known why himself.

"Ah—she thought you might enjoy meeting Mrs. Baddeley."

His uncle drew a long puff on his pipe. "I did. Though that lady's manners are no match for her celebrated beauty."

Nigel nodded.

"My boy, tell me more about these prowlers and burglars. Madame sets a fine table, but her silver is not worth being hanged for, and her jewels are probably paste, as she seems too shrewd to bother with the real ones. What else does she have that is worth stealing?"

Nigel drew a deep breath and plunged in. "Not jewels or silver, but information. A certain young lady has become the subject of a foolish bet."

"Oh, you mean Phoebe. Heard about that from my valet." The earl managed to puff and chuckle at the same time. "Don't know why she didn't tell me."

"You know of it?"

"All of London knows. What nonsense. I don't care if Phoebe wears an Invisible Arrangement or not. Certainly most of what I see must be real—it barely stays inside her bodice. No, no, it doesn't matter to me."

Nigel could not quite comprehend his uncle's nonchalance.

"I only wish she had come to me as soon as she knew," Bertie said, still chuckling. "I could have defended her honor—well, no. I am too old to fight duels at dawn. The grass is very damp in the morning. Brings on the gout."

"I suppose it does." So all of his heroics had been for nothing, Nigel reflected. Well, not quite for nothing. Miss Mousey had appreciated his efforts last night—was it only last night? He wondered if Sheridan had woken up yet and if the man remembered his foolish adventure. All to win a bet that would not be won and no longer mattered.

Nigel went over the particulars, remembering the delicious feeling of holding Isabelle close when she had been so frightened. He would do it all over again, he knew, although a sword might be a more dashing weapon than a broken poker.

"It was Madame Zazou's notebook that they wanted, Uncle. And they did get it—but it was written in code, so they brought it back."

His uncle puffed away. "All's well that ends well."

"Perhaps. Am I to understand that you intend to marry Phoebe, whether she wears an Arrangement or not?"

"Pooh—women must have their little secrets. Her corsets and drawers and so forth are her own affair. As I have said, it is my health that concerns me, and Phoebe has given me no cause for alarm on that score."

Nigel chose not to repeat Jeremy's suspicions. His duty as a nephew had been done.

"That Miss Mousey is a delightful gel. She seems to have taken your fancy. Did you say where she was from?"

"I did not," Nigel said in a level tone. "I know very little about her."

"Hm." He puffed silently and his nephew watched the smoke ascend as before. "Do you want to know more?"

"Yes." Nigel left out his other thoughts on the subject, lest his uncle think he had lost his wits and his heart simultaneously. *I want to know more, because I want to love her and only her. I want to marry her. I want to roll around with her all night long in a gigantic bed carved with cupids and not get up until afternoon.* That would require a great deal more explaining than he was ready to do, and he was not yet sure of the lady's feelings toward him.

Fortunately, his uncle changed the subject. "Lord Charles asked after you."

Nigel had been hoping he wouldn't. "Well, what did Papa have to say?"

"That he would be damned—something something—that you were an ungrateful something else—or something like that."

"The usual."

"Quite." His uncle let out a small puff of smoke, then inhaled again and blew smoke rings, sending small ones through the larger. "That used to amuse you tremendously, Nigel."

"It still does." He smiled at his uncle.

Bertie waved the rings away and changed the subject. "Back to Miss Mousey. Wherever did you find her?"

"Here," Nigel replied.

"She lives here?"

"She is Madame Zazou's assistant."

His uncle puffed and pondered that for a few seconds without replying. "But she seems to be an educated woman."

Jeremy opened the French doors and popped his head out just in time to overhear the latter part of the conversation. He came out onto the balcony, closing the doors behind him.

"She is indeed. And well able to make me look like a fool. Why is she making stays and trimming drawers, Nigel? You must know more about her than you let on. At least she seems to look to you often, or in your direction, since you quitted the table."

Nigel merely shrugged, though he was secretly pleased to hear this.

"She ought to be a governess for some rich man's brats—or at least a rich man's mistress," his friend added. "Dash it, she is very pretty and damnably intelligent."

"Watch what you say, Jeremy." Nigel's tone was level, but there was a warning in his eyes.

"Now, now," Bertie said. "Jeremy meant no harm. Shall we go in? My pipe has gone out and I am experiencing a chill."

The three men left the balcony and resumed their positions at the dining table. Jeremy picked up the decanter to pour himself yet another glass of wine, which he tossed down his throat in one go.

"Being a governess is a perfectly respectable calling, Nigel. As for the rest—forgive me. I did not mean to imply that the young lady of whom we were speaking was less than chaste."

Grace giggled. "You chased me last night, Jemmy. Round and round the bed."

"I am talking about a different word altogether. You would not know what I mean."

"Oh." She pouted prettily and played with the diamond drops that decorated her earlobes. "So you think me stupid, do you?"

"No. You are quite shrewd in your way," Jeremy replied honestly. "But hardly educated."

"I know what I need to know, and that is enough for me."

Her lover smiled indulgently. "And for me as well."

She rose rather unsteadily. "I must repair to the necessary."

Jeremy gave her an affectionate slap upon the rump as she left. Nigel frowned. Grace was a strumpet, to be sure, but she was a very successful one, and it seemed to him that Jeremy should treat her with somewhat more respect.

Isabelle was doing her best to remain upright, but Nigel thought it wise to take Jeremy's seat. The object of his most tender affections had clearly had far too much wine.

Madame returned and several more courses followed. When justice had been done to the excellent dinner, she rang for help and the dishes were quickly cleared away.

The guests remained in their chairs, replete with food and wine and feeling very merry indeed. Grace returned and collapsed into the chair next to Jeremy, now on the opposite side of the table from Isabelle. Nigel fixed him with what he hoped was an intimidating stare and sat very straight.

The old earl rested his elbows upon the damask tablecloth, in the way of one too content to care much about manners for the moment.

"You set a fine table, Madame Zazou. I have not had such delicious fare since I was last in Paris. And that was many years ago."

"You are most kind." Madame gave him a doe-eyed look from under her lashes. The wine had brought a sparkle to her dark eyes and a youthful flush to her cheeks.

Bertie harrumphed, looking again at her décolletage but looking longer. Isabelle and Nigel exchanged a smile, and Jeremy glanced round to see what had amused them so.

"Well—I suppose coffee will be next," the writer said expectantly.

"It will be served in the drawing room, Monsieur Gresham."

Jeremy nudged his drowsy mistress, who had begun to lean on him again. "Grace—dearest Mrs. Baddeley—do not doze off."

"Hm?" She sat up straight and looked about her. "Oh dear—I beg everybody's pardon."

"Have you no amusing gossip, Grace? It is the duty of ladies to provide it, you know, for the entertainment of all."

This remark and his condescending tone piqued Isabelle no end. "Is that so, Mr. Gresham? Even if the gentlemen are dull?"

Jeremy's eyes lit up. There was nothing he liked more than a battle of wits, and he was not likely to get it from the rest of the company. And why was Nigel looking at him like that?

"I beg your pardon, my dear Miss Mousey, if I have bored you."

Nigel tossed his serviette upon the table. "You have rather monopolized the conversation, Jeremy."

"Do you mean that others do not find me as fascinating as I find myself?" the other man asked wryly. "I humbly beg your forgiveness."

"Well, you have a way with words," Bertie said. "But I do hope that this evening will not be mentioned in next week's *Tatler*."

"I do not contribute to that publication, sir," Jeremy said.

"Why not?" Isabelle asked pertly.

"They do not pay enough. I make more money from my own broadsides and scandal sheets."

She nodded, wondering if she had read any of these. If she had, his name had not appeared on them. "What else do you publish?"

"Oh—novels. The sort that young ladies consume by the dozen but never admit to reading."

"And do young ladies write them as well?" Isabelle inquired.

"Sometimes. But I have myself authored many, under the *nom de plume* of Amelia Holdfast."

Grace laughed immoderately. "Are you Amelia Holdfast, then? You never told me that, Jemmy."

"We seldom discuss literature, my dear," he said patiently.

Bertie banged a fist on the table in an amiable way, but he made the glasses jump. "I say—that is most amusing, my good man. My fiancée, Miss Sharpe, will read nothing but Amelia Holdfast romances," he added. "She enjoys them immensely and will be tickled to find that I have met the author."

Madame put a hand upon his arm and let it linger there for a few seconds. "But you will not tell her you have dined with me, *m'sieu*."

The old earl turned redder than her gown. "No, no—of course not."

Isabelle did not feel at all sorry for Phoebe, though she supposed she ought to. "Miss Sharpe is more concerned with her appearance than anything else," she whispered to Nigel. "Your uncle deserves better. He is a warm-hearted old fellow."

Nigel looked at her with astonishment. Isabelle had never talked to him with quite that degree of freedom.

Jeremy addressed his next remark to the earl. "Miss Sharpe is a beauty and no mistake—but I have heard she has a fiery temper."

"She does."

*"Saepe creat molles aspera spina rosas,"* Jeremy said after a moment's thought.

The old earl howled with glee and banged his fist on the table again. "Well said! That ought to be her motto."

Nigel sighed. "Jeremy, do not spout Latin. The ladies do not understand it."

"I do," said Isabelle suddenly. "It is from Ovid. 'A sharp thorn may make delicate roses.' "

Jeremy looked at her curiously and the earl applauded. "Three cheers for Miss Mousey! You are a clever girl!"

"And where did you learn Latin, if I may ask?" Jeremy's voice was suddenly soft.

"Oh—here and there," Isabelle said diffidently. She twirled a loose lock of hair around one finger and looked him straight in the eye.

"Not here, certainly. Unless you are something other than a staymaker's assistant."

She stared him down. "That is for me to know and you to find out."

Grace frowned. "Jemmy, stop. Miss Mousey does not have to answer your stupid questions."

"I don't mind. Fire away." Isabelle was feeling bold indeed.

"Well, I suppose anyone might memorize a quotation or two, even a woman. Try this, then. *Mus non uni fidit antro.*"

Isabelle worked it out in her head. " 'A mouse does not put its faith in only one mousehole'—is that right?"

"Yes," said Jeremy, "and might I ask where you would run to next? Where are you from, Miss Mousey?"

He had trapped her as deftly as a waiting cat. Isabelle could not find the words to lie. And for a wonder, she no longer wanted to. If Madame's guests—if Nigel, the only one who was important to her—did not accept her for who she was, or comprehend that coincidence had brought her here and friendship had caused her to remain—

then they could go to the devil and waste not a minute in doing so.

"I am from Surrey. The Priory, to be exact, near—" She named the village, to Nigel's great surprise. "Hang it—I shall tell all. Yes, I am more than a stay-maker's assistant . . . but Madame Zazou has been a true friend to me and I shall be forever in her debt." This thought caused a small but highly sentimental tear to roll down her pretty cheek.

"Do continue. And have some more wine!" Jeremy picked up the decanter but Nigel made him set it down.

She finished what was left in her glass before Nigel could take it away as well.

"Isabelle, are you sure that you want to reveal your secrets here?" he asked nervously.

She hiccupped. "Why not? I have done nothing wrong and it is not as if I have gone on the town or taken a lover."

Jeremy's eyes were bright with interest, Nigel noticed with dismay.

"Is Miss Mousey your real name?" Jeremy asked.

She nodded. "I am the ward and d-distant relation of Lady Griselda Sneyd."

Bertie looked suddenly alarmed but Isabelle took no notice and went on.

"How did you come to London?" Jeremy inquired.

"I was su-supposed to stay with her friend, the duke of Numbumberland."

Jeremy thought it over. "I expect she means the duke of Southumberland."

"But Oswald died two years ago," Bertie said wonderingly.

"So I found out. But not until the c-coachman who brought me here abandoned me on the street, and a cutpurse left me p-penniless." Another tear rolled down her cheek. Her woes suddenly seemed too much to bear, but a small voice in her head told her that the wine had gotten the better of her.

Madame murmured assent. "It is true. Then she met me. Her story touched me and I took her in." She seemed on the verge of weeping herself.

The earl whipped out a handkerchief embroidered with a crest and offered it to her. "There, there. Do not cry, Madame."

The Frenchwoman took the handkerchief and dabbed daintily at her tears. Isabelle had never thought it possible to look elegant while crying but Madame Zazou managed this feat with ease.

"There, there." Bertie patted Madame on the back in a shockingly familiar way as he said this. Nigel and Isabelle could not help staring at them, which Jeremy could not help noticing.

"Dear me. So many raised eyebrows and sideways glances. We shall have no need of words if this keeps up."

"Then change the subject, Jem," Nigel said rather sharply. He would have done so himself if he were not so flabbergasted by Miss Mousey's revelation.

"Ah—it would be difficult to come up with anything as fascinating as Miss Mousey's tale, Nigel. I would pay her for the right to publish it myself."

"You shall do no such thing. And do not put her into an Amelia Holdfast novel, or I shall really have to thrash you this time."

Jeremy waved away this threat. "You are always saying that. But her story is remarkably affecting. All it needs is a dashing highwayman, a carriage chase, and a wedding in the village church. The reading public would be agog."

Isabelle sighed. "There will be no wedding. Because of my f-foolishness, I might never marry! What man would want such a headstrong hussy for a wife?"

"An excellent title!" Jeremy crowed. *"The Headstrong Hussy!"*

Her eyes began to fill with tears again. "I only wanted to stay in London for as long as I could. I— I was not thinking of the consequences."

Grace Baddeley nodded understandingly. "When I went on the town, I felt much the same."

"But Miss Mousey is not on the town, my dear Grace," Jeremy said swiftly. "There is a world of difference between your experience and hers, and perhaps the less said about all that, the better."

Isabelle did not want to look at Nigel. She supposed he had thought her innocent but no longer did.

Nigel wanted only for her to stop crying. Most assuredly she had not done anything to be ashamed of.

But if he could prevail upon Madame Zazou to declare the dinner officially over—and if the guests could be persuaded to do without the coffee and Turkish delights—perhaps nothing more would be said that was sure to be deeply regretted come the morning.

# CHAPTER 18

*The morning after . . .*

*Clink.* A pebble hit the window. Isabelle cracked open one eye. The noise was enough to shatter her ears, though the windowpane seemed intact. Alas, she was suffering from the headache to end all headaches, a just retribution for last night and payment in advance for a lifetime's worth of sins.

Why, oh why, had she let Jeremy Gresham pour her so much wine? It had caused her to pour out her feelings just as freely and her life story as well. She would never live it down.

She would never drink wine again. She would never consort with writers. She would enter a nunnery, if there were any left in England, as soon as she got up.

*Clink.* Another pebble followed the first. She crawled out of bed and walked slowly to the window, glad that the dawn was overcast and a soft spring rain was falling. She stood behind the curtain and peeped out.

There was Nigel, standing below her window.

"Isabelle!" His voice sounded almost—adoring. Damn him. She was in no mood to be adored, for she did not deserve to be adored.

If she knew when the post coach left for Surrey, she would be on it straightaway. Or perhaps she should compose the sequel to her life story in a Grub Street attic, as Lady Griselda would no doubt disown her.

She could see the title, in gilt lettering on blue buckram, hovering before her bleary eyes. *The Headstrong Hussy Heads Home.* Oh, damn Jeremy, while she was at it.

"Isabelle!" Nigel called, somewhat less adoringly.

She flung open the sash and hissed at him to be quiet.

"There you are, my dearest. You look enchanting!" This was not even remotely true but he thought she needed to hear it. He blew her a kiss.

She rubbed her temples. "Oh—my head!"

"You must not drink so much wine, dearest. It does not agree with you."

"Thank you for sharing that advice with the entire street, Nigel!"

A passing chimneysweep gave her a broad smile, his teeth white in his sooty face. Nigel reached into his pocket and gave him a few coins for luck.

"Thank you, sir. And you there!" The sweep waved at Isabelle. "Himself is right about the wine. Stick to gin, I always say." He went on his way, whistling.

"I am on my way to my uncle's apartments, Isabelle. But I wanted to say good morning."

She looked at him through half-closed eyes, her head throbbing. "Have you forgotten last night? Did I not confess who I was? Why are you here?"

"Because I—because I wanted to see you first thing. But you are in no condition to receive callers. Go back to bed." He blew her another kiss.

Isabelle slammed down the sash. Clearly he was mad—or she was dreaming. Possibly her confession had unhinged his mind. Certainly it had changed everything. She crawled back into bed and pulled the covers up over her head.

His uncle's cook prepared breakfast as requested and served it forth in the drawing room. Nigel sat on the edge of the Moorish divan, not wanting to stretch out as before. Poached eggs were best eaten in an upright position, being wont to slide off the toast.

He peppered and salted the two upon his plate and made short work of them. His uncle contented himself with coffee and a small apple.

"I ate too much at Madame Zazou's." He sighed lugubriously. "But it was worth it. I would not wish to offend such a charming woman. The food was excellent and so was the wine."

The younger man swallowed his last bite of egg. "It was a most interesting dinner."

Bertie nodded and yawned. "Miss Mousey's confession was the high point. I thought Jeremy's idea to turn it into a book was most amusing."

Nigel scowled. "Left to his own devices, he would."

"The gel gave me quite a start when she mentioned her guardian. If that is the Lady Griselda I know, of the Shropshire Sneyds—" He broke off.

His nephew set down his plate and stretched out to digest.

"Is it a long story?"

"It is."

"I am ready to hear it."

His uncle settled deeper into the capacious armchair he preferred. "Griselda was a busybody and a bluestocking, and much given to moralizing."

"Go on."

"However, she had a curious habit of taking things that did not belong to her. After every house party to which she was invited, there would be silver missing, or a small piece of jewelry. Or some such thing."

Nigel rubbed his chin thoughtfully—he had not yet shaved. "I see."

"And so she was left out more often than not and became a social pariah of sorts."

The manservant bustled in to remove the breakfast tray. "More coffee, my lord?"

"No, though it is excellent," the earl said mournfully. "But I fear I am suffering from a creeping dyspepsia, which coffee aggravates. It is hovering near my ankles and will move upward in due time."

"There is no such ailment, Uncle." Nigel watched the manservant leave with the tray. He would not have minded more coffee but did not think to ask for it.

Bertie looked offended. "I have unshakable faith in my physician, and he has diagnosed it."

"Then he is a charlatan."

The older man was silent for a long while. "Perhaps it is simply age. Ah, well. I should not be thinking of marrying so young a woman. Phoebe may be too much for me."

Nigel gave him a sympathetic look. "Never."

"Madame Zazou said—well, never mind. I was explaining about Lady Griselda."

He would not mind hearing about both, Nigel realized. But perhaps Griselda's tale had the most bearing on his future with Miss Mousey. He would ask his uncle what Madame Zazou had said later.

"As I was saying, she seemed to be a thief in a small way, though so clever it could never be proved. It made no sense, for she had inherited some money—perhaps insufficient to buy the little things she wanted or cover her gambling debts.

"She liked to play at cards in secret but she always lost—was fleeced more than once, as I remember. And she herself was not exactly pretty, though her figure was handsome when she was in her twenties. That was years ago. Time and gravity lie in wait for us all," Bertie said gloomily.

"Never mind that," Nigel said. "Is she a relative of Miss Mousey? No one I know seems to have heard of the family."

Bertie shrugged. "I remember a few, but not well. Perhaps they died out."

Nigel had thought more than once that her parents could not possibly be alive. But there were many pieces to the puzzle that was Isabelle, and he was not likely to find them all right away.

Isabelle was no doubt sound asleep. He thought fondly of her disheveled appearance at the window and how fiercely she had scowled. But the love he felt for her made her lovely in his eyes— and a morning's rest would do wonders for her disposition.

"What else do you know about Lady Griselda, Uncle?"

The older man hesitated. "There is more. But it is highly personal in nature."

"I will keep whatever you say in strictest confidence."

"See that you do." And his uncle began to explain. . . .

# CHAPTER 19

*No price too high . . .*

Nigel's next stop, once he was respectably dressed, was his solicitor's offices at the Inns of Court. Armed with some very interesting information, thanks to his uncle, he took a hackney cab thence, and arrived early.

He spied Mr. Boggles immediately upon the fellow's somewhat tardy arrival. He was laden as always with several thick books, somberly dressed in black superfine and down-at-heel shoes. They went inside together, but Nigel came out alone.

The case was extremely complicated, and Mr. Boggles needed at least a week and a breathtaking fee in advance to take it on.

This Nigel provided cheerfully, astonishing the old solicitor, who seemed to be expecting the usual complaints. But no price was too great to ensure that Isabelle might be his someday—and that

she might come into what was rightfully hers,
Nigel thought.

Two weeks later, for Nigel had begun to complain at last, Mr. Boggles showed him in to his cobwebby office once more and invited him to sit down.

The old man opened a large book, bound in pebbled black leather that had worn to soft brown along the edges and spine, and flipped through several pages until he found the one he wanted.

"In the case of Miss Mousey," he began, pausing to peer over his crooked spectacles at Nigel, "it seems that her lineage is indeed distinguished. And there is valuable land and other assets to which she might have rights, though much of the estate has been sold off or lost to the vagaries of Lady Luck, to say nothing of Lady Griselda. There are entails too complex to explain and mortgages older than Methuselah, and spurious claims by dubious cousins, and so forth."

"Dubious claims by spurious cousins. I see," said Nigel, not seeing at all. However, he would let the old solicitor ramble on for a while longer.

"However, if a suit were to be brought in Chancery to look into the matter, Miss Mousey may well come into a fortune, since all her sanguinary relations are unfortunately in a state of permanent demise."

"Do you mean they are dead, Mr. Boggles?"

The older man paused to wipe his spectacles on his waistcoat. "That is what I mean, yes. She is alone in the world. Her so-called great-aunt is not even her legal guardian, let alone a near and dear relation."

Nigel thought about that. So he would not have to ask a beetle-browed papa for her hand. This was a very good thing. "Do continue."

Mr. Boggles cleared his throat. "Perhaps you are familiar with Aesop's fables—do you remember the story of the mouse who pulled a thorn from a lion's paw?"

Nigel nodded. "I do."

"The obliging rodent was rewarded with the lion's favor. And long ago, a distant ancestor of Miss Mousey who was a court jester to the glorious and celebrated King Richard, known as the Lion-hearted—"

"Yes, yes, get on with it, Mr. Boggles. What thorn did the first Mousey pull from the royal paw?"

The old solicitor smiled, creasing his face into thousands of wrinkles. "As he capered in bells and motley, and told bawdy jokes, the king forgot his troubles. For that, the jester was amply rewarded and married off to a duke's sister, a woman so wanton she once dallied with a monk—"

"Surely the church records made no mention of that. Are you inventing this wild tale, Mr. Boggles? I am not amused."

Mr. Boggles turned faintly red. "No, sir, I am not. Another monk scribbled something to that effect in the decorated border of the register. The friars of old were apt to add spiteful comments in the margins, in Latin, which I read, as you know."

"Fascinating. Well, the life of a celibate is full of frustration, I should think. Do go on."

"Isabelle's direct ancestors married into the family much later, of course. But the original Mouseys were blessed with numerous progeny and their descendants can be found in the greatest houses of

England to this day." He squinted at his notes. "One was wed to a Catt, but the marriage had no issue. Interesting."

"Indeed it is, Mr. Boggles."

"Over time, some ascended into the ranks of the minor peers and some made fortunes. However humble their beginnings, the family prospered."

Nigel waved his hand impatiently. "Yet their descendants squandered their patrimony and mismanaged the ancestral estates. They are rich in land and little else."

Mr. Boggles looked momentarily astonished. "Those were my next words, sir. How did you know—"

"I looked at your notes."

The older man folded his hands over his black silk waistcoat and sighed. "Then you also know how much work it will be to regain Miss Mousey's inheritance. She might not see a penny of it for a year or more."

"All the more reason to marry her immediately. She can spend my money in the meantime, to her heart's content. I mean to make her happy, Boggles, very happy indeed. She shall not wait another day."

The old man polished his spectacles and pored over his notes once more. "Very odd that Lady Griselda was able to access funds in trust. She is not really a Mousey at all, as I said—some irregularities in the marriage records shall have to be corrected. No, she is merely a Sneyd, of the Shropshire Sneyds. Her mother was a Croaker until she married a Huff and then a Sneyd—"

"Please write it all down. My head is spinning."

"Very good, sir. I shall do that. And if the young

lady requests it, I shall look into filing a suit on her behalf."

"Thank you, Mr. Boggles."

At that moment, Isabelle was enjoying a late breakfast at the house on Clarges Street with Madame and Jehane, who had come downstairs for the occasion, accompanied by Fig.

They were sipping coffee and being entertained by Jeremy, who had decided to pay an impromptu morning call upon his new favorite ladies, who were excellent listeners. Madame occasionally translated for Jehane's benefit, and the breakfast room rang with the old lady's silvery laugh.

The maid peeped in and announced Nigel's arrival. Isabelle heard him bound upstairs to join the merry group of friends, where he was always welcome.

"What news?" Jeremy asked in the stentorian tone of a Shakespearean actor.

"Mr. Boggles has explained everything. Isabelle, did you know that you are—or will be—a rich woman?"

She shrugged, assuming he was joking. "Jeremy says the same, if I will only embellish my life story as he recommends."

"Yes. Though it has nearly everything—passion, wit, a noble hero, and a beautiful heroine. There is also a plot of sorts, so that the reader may easily tell the beginning from the end. However, the story still lacks a carriage chase and a moral."

"Is that so very important in these times, Jeremy?" Madame inquired.

"*Certainement,*" he said grandly, mispronouncing

the French word. "Conscientious mamas will not buy a book without a moral for their darling daughters. However, they will read it themselves, cover to cover, just to be sure the story has no redeeming virtues whatsoever."

"Of course," said Isabelle. "I always do."

Nigel smiled down at her. "As far as plots, there are some interesting new developments in your story."

"Well, tell us, Nigel," said Jeremy impatiently.

Nigel sat down and related all of what Mr. Boggles had said, clarifying a few points where he could and leaving out Aesop's fable.

The group sat in silence for at least a minute.

"That is wonderful news indeed, *chérie*," said Madame, very softly. "But we will be so sad when you leave us."

"I shall never go far away, Madame. You have become my family. I have no other."

Jehane whispered something to her daughter, who nodded.

"Maman wants to know what will become of Lady Griselda."

Isabelle just shook her head. "I cannot change the past, or what she has done. But I intend to forgive her as she is very old. And I will provide a pension and a snug cottage with servants so that she may live out her few years in comfort."

Even cynical Jeremy was impressed. "They say that revenge is a dish best eaten cold—of course it can do wonders for an overheated plot. But you have chosen a most gracious way to close that chapter of your life. I applaud you, Miss Mousey."

They all applauded her but she held up a hand to stop them.

"However, I think I might amuse myself at her expense just once and that will be my revenge. I will never entirely forgive her for the curates."

Nigel looked a little puzzled. "You have told us much of your life in Surrey but you did not mention curates. Be so good as to explain, my dear."

Isabelle began. "Lady Griselda spent much of her time and my money entertaining young clergymen, with an eye to my eventual marriage."

"I see," Jeremy said. "And did you fancy any?"

Isabelle shook her head. "I despised them all equally. They were pale and fretful and fearful of committing the smallest sin. The most innocent remarks caused them to hem and haw and dart looks everywhere but upon me. I found their company most trying."

Though Nigel was secure in the affections of his beloved, he could not hide his pleasure upon hearing this.

"I love only one man—and he is by my side."

The group applauded again. Then Madame rose from the table, motioning to Jeremy to go, and led her mother slowly from the room. "It is time we left these two alone, *n'est-ce pas?*"

"Damn," Jeremy sighed. "But she has not explained her plan to give Lady Griselda a taste of her own medicine. I cannot rest until I know how it ends, Madame."

The Frenchwoman took him by the arm. "We will know soon enough. Come."

# CHAPTER 20

*O happy day!*

They had been some minutes in each other's arms, as nearly as that affectionate state could be achieved in the small chairs of the breakfast room. Nigel spoke at last.

"My dear Isabelle, you know something of the world without having been sullied by it in any way. For all the notoriety attached to her name, Madame Zazou has watched over you carefully. Though I myself have a reputation as a rake—"

"Do you deserve it?" Isabelle asked pertly.

"There are some questions a wise man does not answer. Will it be enough if I am devoted to you?"

"Yes," she replied simply, twining her arms about his neck and nestling into his shoulder.

"I am weary of the fashionable world and its so-called pleasures. I long for a family—for a wife. For you, Isabelle."

She opened her mouth to speak but Nigel forged ahead, hoping she would not argue or ask too many questions.

"I cannot follow custom and ask your great-aunt for your hand in marriage, as it would be a sham. Unless there is a male relative—" Mr. Boggles had said there were none but Nigel wanted to be quite sure.

"There is not. Are you proposing, Mr. Wollaston?" said Isabelle.

"I am, Miss Mousey. If you will have me, we will wed."

"I have not made my debut."

He nodded. "A minor detail. Bertie would be happy to present you at the Court of St. James. You need not weary yourself with an endless round of balls and assemblies and tedious calls upon other ladies."

Isabelle looked at him indignantly, recovering her wits. "What if I want to go to balls and breakfasts and call upon people? I have yet to enjoy the pleasures of society, and you will not confine me to any house, however splendid, until I experience these delights for myself."

Nigel sighed and gave her a long, deeply affectionate look. "Might I suggest that you enter the ballroom upon the arm of your newly-wedded husband? Would you like to pay calls in a pretty phaeton all your own or arrive in Madame's black carriage with Alf?"

"I should prefer to arrive with Alf," she said impudently. "And do not forget Robert."

"Very well. Then I shall hire them both. Madame Zazou will never forgive me."

Isabelle wanted to laugh. How far would he go to get her to say yes?

"I cannot take Alf away from his brother. He would not go."

"He need not go far, my darling. My uncle wants to purchase a house for us close by. He has looked at one that he says is too big for him, though just the right size for newlyweds who plan to start a family."

"Hm. I will have to look at it myself."

He sighed. "Of course, Isabelle. As you are soon to be rich, you do not need me or anybody else. You can tell me to go to the devil if you like."

"But I do need you, Nigel. And I love you. With all my heart."

"Then nothing more needs to be said."

And nothing was, for a long and pleasurable while. . . .

Somewhat later that day, Miss Phoebe Sharpe arrived to begin the fittings for her trousseau, accompanied by her footman, Tomkyns, as before.

Isabelle watched from an upstairs room as the two of them came up the stairs, not knowing or caring where they would go next, as she was no longer working for Madame.

She heard the usual commotion downstairs and returned to her book, an Amelia Holdfast novel with an unusually silly heroine. She would have to have a word with Jeremy—she could write a much better book with ease. Perhaps the members of White's would wager on that. Isabelle knew who would win.

* * *

Madame was busy with other customers, and Phoebe was shown into a small sitting room by a flustered new maid, who did not have the sense to ask the footman to wait downstairs.

He entered with her and stood by impassively, watching Phoebe shrug out of her light shawl and put down her fan and reticule. She did not mind if he stayed. Tomkyns was a man of few words, and three of those were *yes, your ladyship*, which was something she found most agreeable.

They might have a bit of fun for a few moments until she was called, and no one would be the wiser. She pushed him into a chair and perched herself upon his knee, undoing his buttons one by one. . . .

Shortly thereafter, Bertie strolled by the house on Clarges Street upon his daily constitutional, as recommended by his physician. He had taken to calling upon Madame now and then since the night of the dinner, though that dear lady was often busy.

But he did not mind waiting in her pretty drawing room, and she always found time to speak with him most warmly, now that their families were to be joined in matrimony.

He could grow quite fond of the beautiful French-woman if he was not careful, he reflected. As the drawing room was presently occupied by waiting clients who were having tea, the same new maid who had seen to Phoebe and Tomkyns waved the earl to the same room, assuming that they were gone.

Bertie entered. They were not.

"I am undone!" Phoebe cried.

"No, you are unbuttoned. And so is your footman. Please do not try to explain." Bertie bowed ever so slightly to her. "And might I add, Miss Sharpe, that this is the unkindest cut of all." He withdrew and went in search of Madame Zazou.


Nigel was not at all surprised to hear of this some hours later, though he did think a dalliance with a footman was stooping rather low.

His uncle seemed unconcerned. "I had my doubts all along, my boy. And by the way, Madame Zazou and I have come to an agreement that will benefit us both. The details I shall keep to myself, but suffice it to say that she understands me and I understand her. I think we shall find happiness together."

Somehow, Nigel did not find that surprising either. The earl had evidently been thinking about a lot of things, considering what he said next.

"Your father will break his neck eventually, considering how badly he rides, or expire from apoplexy. And you may well be the earl, when you are young enough to enjoy it. Miss Mousey, a countess—imagine it!"

"I cannot."

"Failing that, I have made arrangements to settle a considerable sum upon you, my boy. You are expected to enjoy it. And I hope that you will provide me with great-nephews and great-nieces who will make the rafters ring."

"You have no rafters," Nigel observed.

"I must. Can't have a house without rafters. But the children cannot disturb my afternoon slumbers."

"We shall see to it, Uncle," Nigel said with a wink.


Isabelle penned a letter that was sure to bring Lady Griselda out of Surrey at last—with help from Jeremy, who shamelessly added lurid details that made her blush.

One week later, as arranged by James upon the old footman's customary journey to London, she heard the familiar creak of the Priory's ancient carriage. Her so-called aunt had arrived right on time, and Isabelle was ready to play the part of a ravished innocent, wearing a pink morning robe over a somewhat revealing nightgown.

There was a scene. Lady Griselda made accusations and pointed fingers, and shrieked her fury at one and all. Then she bundled Isabelle, who sobbed and wrung her hands most convincingly, into the carriage.

"Wanton girl! You shall marry the new vicar after all! If he will have you!"

Lady Griselda almost shoved Isabelle against the squabs. The driver sat on the box high above, the lapels of his greatcoat pulled up over his ears and a battered hat pulled down over his eyes, though the day was quite warm.

He was strongly built and his shoulders were broad. At least he might afford some protection from highwaymen, since Griselda would probably insist upon traveling by back roads to hide Isabelle's ignominious return from village gossips.

"You ungrateful girl! Sharper than a serpent's tooth, you are! You have disgraced the noble name of Mousey!"

Isabelle wanted to cry, but the tears would not come. Perhaps she simply did not want to give her great-aunt the satisfaction of seeing her sorrow. It was quite a performance, watched by a crowd in the street, who commented as noisily on the action as if it were taking place in a theatre. She stared dully out the window, watching them watch her.

Lady Griselda got in and fell back against the squabs, wheezing a little. "Not a word! Not a word from you, my gel!"

Isabelle compressed her lips and glared at her great-aunt.

"Such a black look! Your expression is quite fierce! I will not countenance such impertinence!"

She obeyed and turned her face into the cushions, grateful for a way to hide her smile.

They had traveled several hours when the coach suddenly came to a halt. Lady Griselda was thrown back hard, which made her wheeze again.

"What the devil? What happened? Has a wheel cracked?"

There was a sound of sliding from above, and one of the men on the box jumped down. He opened the door. Isabelle was not surprised to see that it was the coachman, still bundled up to his ears, a thick scarf over his mouth.

He said something. His voice was muffled—but oh, the familiar sound of it thrilled her heart. "Sand and liver!"

"What? What on earth did he say?"

Nigel—for it was he, clad in the coachman's old coat from Madame Zazou's house—pulled down the scarf around his face. "I said . . . stand and deliver!"

Lady Griselda shrieked. "James! James! Save us!

We have fallen into the hands of robbers! Isabelle—give him your jewels! Mine are worth more!"

Nigel reached out a hand and helped Isabelle out of the coach with gentlemanly aplomb.

"Isabelle! Do not go with him! He will take your greatest treasure!—Well, I suppose that is already gone. Oh, where is James?"

"Right 'ere, your ladyship," came a cheerful shout from atop the coach.

"James! Can you not do something? Bash him! Break his nose!"

There was a pause, while she waited for a reply.

"He is bigger than me. And younger. No, I think I shall remain where I am."

While this discussion was taking place, Isabelle went straight into Nigel's arms and stayed there.

"Isabelle! What are you doing? Have you no shame?"

Isabelle shook her head and nestled closer. "None at all, Aunt."

Lady Griselda took stock of the situation and evidently decided that the time had come for shrewd negotiations. "You!" She waggled an imperious finger at Nigel.

Nigel only raised an eyebrow in reply.

"We are gentlewomen, sir! Unhand that girl! I will defend her virtue with my last breath, and my own!"

Nigel merely grinned. "You have no virtue to defend, dear lady."

"What? How can you say such things!" Lady Griselda was nearly hysterical.

Nigel shook his head. "It is you who are robbing Isabelle and not I. An investigation has commenced

into the particulars, but she is not your poor relation. And I am not a highwayman. I am here to see
that justice is done and the truth told."

The old lady's small mouth opened into a wrin-
kled O.

"Do you remember your third and final season,
Lady Griselda? You had been on the shelf too long
when you decided to seduce the Honorable Bertram
Wollaston, the future Earl of Skipwith, who was then
a mere boy of seventeen. You were twenty-five. And
he never forgot your kindness—or your amorous
expertise. You are—or were—the wanton one, not
Isabelle."

"Oh! Oh! I am betrayed! James! James!"

"Yes, your ladyship?"

"Drive on! Save me!"

The old footman took up the reins and watched
Nigel slam the door. It was fortunate that her ladyship chose that moment to swoon.

The footman tipped his hat. "Are ye to be married then, sir?"

Nigel swept up his dearest, laughing with joy, in
his arms. "Yes! By special license. My dear old
uncle has arranged it with Bishop Freamington
and all is in readiness. Dear old Freamy. They were
at Cambridge together, you know."

"Well, then! Come to the Priory in a few months.
Give the old girl a cottage to sulk in and a new curate to fatten up, and she'll be right as rain soon
enough. But—oh, Miss Isabelle. . . ."

"Yes, James?"

"Mrs. Pursley would give anything to see ye wed.
May I bring her to the church?"

"Of course! Here are the directions." Nigel pulled

a piece of paper from his pocket. "And make sure that her ladyship is given a sleeping draught immediately upon her return. For her nerves."

He looked down the road to see the second carriage. Alf and Gabriel were up on the box, with Madame and Jehane and Bertie and Freamy and Robert and Fig, all waving wildly out the window—except Fig, who barked. Grace and Jeremy followed them in a phaeton, driving at a breakneck pace.

James tipped his hat again and set it well back on his head. "I take yer meaning, sir. I will see to it."


The impromptu ceremony at the village church was small but interesting, given that the bride wore a *robe de chambre* of pink silk, and the groom, a ragged coachman's coat that had seen better days.

The cleaner village children were pressed into service to strew the rose petals they had hastily gathered, listening with wide eyes as Bishop Freamington winked at Bertie and said the words that united Nigel and Isabelle in holy matrimony, forever and ever, amen.

Mrs. Pursley, who had been fetched from the Priory by James, cried a river of tears into a handkerchief she borrowed from him. The large square of white linen was altogether drenched when all was said and done, and the wedding party walked out into the brilliant sunshine of June.


Nigel drew his new bride down beside him in the sweet-smelling grass of a Surrey meadow, and she nestled her head against his shoulder. The horse wandered off in search of something green to nibble and perhaps hoping to quench its thirst from the stream that bubbled by the hedgerow.

The sound of the wedding feast was but a distant babble—they had made a hasty escape from the striped tent and happy guests.

It was the purest of pleasures to hold Isabelle so close at last. He made no move that might startle her or arouse him. They lay together for a long while under the great, sheltering oak, dappled by the light that filtered through its leaves, in blissful silence. He stirred first.

"My love—" he began.

"Yes, Nigel?" She raised her head to look into his eyes, her honey-colored hair tumbling about her shoulders. He ran an appreciative hand through its silken strands.

"What if someone sees us?"

Isabelle laughed. "I shall not care if they do. My reputation is quite ruined, thanks to you."

"But I have restored it." He pulled her left hand to his lips to kiss the ring upon it—the ring he had given her to be a constant reminder of his love. The sapphire and diamonds twinkled in the sun, but they were not as bright as her eyes, which shone with tears of joy.

"You are an honorable man, Nigel. And I am a happy woman."

"My darling—" he began again.

Isabelle smiled teasingly. "My love, my darling— can you not finish your sentences, my lord?"

He took her into his arms and embraced her almost roughly, rolling her over and underneath him, caressing her with scandalous abandon until she laughed out loud and batted away his eager hands.

He took a deep breath. "My love. My dear. My own." Then he kissed her long and thoroughly, brushed a fingertip over her parted lips, and gazed into her dreamy eyes. "My wife. There is no sweeter word."

# More Regency Romance
# From Zebra